My Favorite Color is
Your Something Blue

Eva Austin

My Favorite Color is Your Something Blue

A Favorite Color Novella

Copyright © 2024 Eva Austin

All rights reserved.

This novel is a work of fiction. Names, characters, places, and incidents are either products of the author's imagination or used fictitiously.

No part of this book may be reproduced, or stored in a retrieval system, or transmitted in any form or by any means, electronic, mechanical, photocopying, recording, or otherwise, without express written permission from the publisher, except for the use of brief quotations in a book review.

Paperback
ISBN: 979-8-9857474-5-4

Ebook
ISBN: 979-8-9857474-4-7

Published by Inevah Press
Edmond, Oklahoma
www.inevahpress.com

For my daughter Ava

You are my sunshine

1

Morgan

"Please, I beg you. I need an ICEE, and there aren't any gas stations out here. You can get blue raspberry and consider it my 'something blue.'"

With the hot sun beating down on my car, I zip around an old pickup truck. Its rusty bumper barely holds on as it putters down the outside lane of I-40.

I grip the steering wheel and shake my head. "Your wedding isn't for two days. Does that mean you also need something old and something new?"

Ava's giggle tinkles through the hands-free system. "Don't worry. My grandma's here, and this rental house is brand new. Old and new, check. So, will you stop? Pretty please?"

The Oklahoma landscape stretches on. I've been on the road for an hour and a half and would love to keep going. Plus, I stopped thirty minutes ago. But this weekend is not about me.

"Of course. Anything for the bride. As long as you don't mind if I'm late."

"Totally fine. Thank you, thank you, thank you. See you at The Meeting House!"

"You got it." The call ends, and my carefully curated road-trip playlist resumes.

I've got this. No problem. The ICEE will be easy. The rest of the weekend? I don't know. The last wedding I went to was a disaster. For me, anyway. I'm only eighteen. How can I already have wedding drama in my life?

I sigh. It won't be so bad.

But Ava's wedding has my mind veering out of its lane and into a minefield of past hurts. For the last hundred miles, I've fought the urge to analyze every detail, and I now have a headache. Ava's one of my oldest friends, never mind that she's a fair bit older than me. She was my first babysitter, neighbor, and close family friend. I want to be here, be present, and be a fabulous bridesmaid. I shove the thoughts away—again —as I exit the highway and head toward Eufaula, Oklahoma, apparently the last of civilization before my destination, a tiny lakeside community called Carlton Landing. I better grab some ibuprofen while I'm at it.

I park outside a small but clean convenience store and head straight to the ICEE machine. Two other girls are already using it, so I snag a cup and wait. There aren't any lids. Super.

These young teens take their sweet time, sharing a whispered conversation. One of them giggles. "Wow, he's *sooo* cute."

The other giggles too.

The guy they're ogling at the coffee station a few paces away is too old for these thirteen-year-olds, but they're not wrong.

Around my age and wearing well-fitted khaki shorts and a casual Hawaiian shirt, he's beach-ready. No, lake-ready, as we're in one of the most centrally located—ahem, *landlocked*—states in the US.

Dark curls fall over his brow as he tugs a coffee cup free. Huh, his ears are pinked. He must've heard the girls' observations. He glances up, gauges their ages, and turns away.

The girls dare each other to go talk to him as he pours coffee. The braver of the two saunters in his direction.

This I've got to see. They've vacated the ICEE machine, so I take my time filling Ava's cup with the frothy blue concoction. That cannot be a natural color.

He slides his phone from his pocket, standing tall—at least six feet. "Hey, babe." He practically purrs as he dumps powdered creamer into his paper cup. Gross.

The girls falter before continuing, giggling all the way. They don't seem too disappointed as they exit the store.

The boy's gaze finds mine, and I bite my lip to hide my smile. Full dark lashes surrounded those deep-brown eyes, and the brows above them narrow like he can't decide whether to frown at me or laugh.

He jumps when his phone rings against his ear.

I laugh outright, and his ears redden further. Smart. Fake phone call. I walk by, ICEE in hand. "Better get that."

"Right." He decides on the frown. "Hey, Mema," he says in a much less sultry voice. Though, it's still a nice voice. "Okay, I'm coming. I was falling asleep, so I stopped for caffeine. I'm close."

I pay for the ICEE, almost wishing he would've chosen the smile and ignored the call. But it's for the best.

As I get to my car, I pause. I forgot the ibuprofen. I swing around, rummaging in my purse to locate the debit card I dropped inside, and crash into someone—a tall someone with khaki shorts and a Hawaiian button-up.

"Watch it," he snaps as we jump back from each other, but not before the ICEE crushes between us and he drops his coffee. My feet are fire and ice.

I shriek.

His coffee has burst open and splashed all over one of my feet, and the blue slush is dripping down onto the other. I kick off my pink flats and shake it from my pale-yellow skirt.

He stands there, arms out to his side, scowling at the stains down his front and the pile of blue ICEE on his sneaker.

The ICEE that splattered on the side of my white car keeps sliding down, leaving faint blue streaks.

He opens his mouth. Closes it. Opens it again.

I wiggle my coffee foot. "You could have scalded me! Watch where you're going."

His mouth flattens into a scowl. "Me? You're the one who ran into me."

"What? I was standing by my car, digging in my purse. You ran into me." I lift the bag, still hooked over my arm, then groan. "It's in my purse."

Still glaring, he starts running his fingers through his hair but remembers they're blue. "I can't believe this day. Six-a.m. flight, eternal layover, lost luggage, and now you." He waves in my direction as if I'm pond scum.

Jerk. I open my mouth, but he shakes the ICEE from his shoe and spins away to go back inside.

I follow him. "How dare you. I didn't do this."

He yanks napkins from a dispenser and dabs at his shirt. "Then why am I wearing the contents of your cup? Who drinks that crap anyway?"

"Who drinks hours-old gas-station coffee? Disgusting." Though, those hours are likely the only thing saving me from second-degree burns.

"Look around." He spreads his arms. "We're in the middle of nowhere. There's not exactly a Starbucks on every corner."

I grab a napkin and brush it down my front. "My skirt is ruined."

"Did you hear me? Lost luggage. I literally have nothing else to wear. And I'm late."

I cross my arms over my chest and nod to the section of gifts and other random items in the corner, particularly the rack under a sign offering T-shirts for less than eight dollars. "Well, I guess you better go shopping."

While he frowns at them, I check my watch, snag another handful of napkins, and walk away.

After purchasing a new ICEE and draining my shoes, I hit the road and let out a pent-up growl as my phone rings. Dad's checking in again. I haven't made many solo road trips. I stab at a button on the dash to answer it.

"Hello," I practically yell.

There's a pause. "Everything okay, honey?"

"Yeah. Someone spilled blue ICEE all over my new skirt and then had the audacity to yell at *me* about it. Ugh."

"What? How did that happen?"

"What happened?" Mom's anxious voice pipes up. "Is Morgan okay?"

The phone echoes as Dad switches to speakerphone, so I launch into a gripe-fest.

When I finish, Mom giggles.

"Mom, it's not funny. This is why I've sworn off dating until I get to college. Boys are idiots, and they're rude. And pushy. Even the cute ones."

"Too true," Dad agrees. He's probably smiling, which further annoys me. "In fact, you shouldn't date until you're thirty."

Mom sings out, "That *is* the agreement you made when you were five."

"I think it was binding," Dad adds.

They're hopeless. "Yeah, sure, Dad." I wiggle. My damp skirt's sticking to my leg. "I need to change."

"I'm sure you can when you get there," Mom says. "We called because Ava's mom said you were running late."

Lord, give me patience. Ava mustn't have informed her erratic mother that she asked me to stop.

"Well, it's Ava's fault. She wanted the ICEE. I'll be there in fifteen minutes."

"Okay, honey. Text us when you get there, and we'll see you for the wedding on Saturday."

"Dad, I just said I'll be there in fifteen minutes. Why do I need to text you in fifteen minutes?"

"That's plenty of time to get in an accident or become stranded or hit a deer or any number of other things."

"Thanks for the happy, reassuring thoughts."

"No problem. Don't forget to text."

"Fine."

"Love you."

"You too."

They hang up, and I force myself to loosen my grip on the steering wheel. I let out a breath. I've got this.

It's smooth sailing from here. The worst is behind me. I just need to get to Carlton Landing and survive a long, hot wedding weekend in the middle of Nowhere, Oklahoma.

No problem.

2

Morgan

Fifteen minutes later, I veer off Highway 9 and through the main entrance to Carlton Landing. Not bad. A low whistle sneaks out. Pretty grand stuff for a lakeside community in the boondocks. Two stately shiplap and honey-wood framed pillars flank the road.

Huh.

My blue-streaked car creeps through a dry forest where red dirt rock and spindly trees fight for real estate alongside a winding, uphill drive. I don't pass a single car and begin to think perhaps this was some sort of joke—just kidding, there aren't any houses back here. Then I crest a hill and roll along near the edge of a cliff overlooking what must be Lake Eufaula far below.

"Oh, wow." I power down my window.

A manicured grassy landing nestles between the cliff's edge and the road, and four white Adirondack chairs form a happy row facing the lake and miles of forest.

I press deeper into my seat, suppressing a strong desire to jump out of my car, run across the grass, and peer over the ledge. Maybe sit a while. Leave my phone in the car. Forget about weddings, past and present.

But I'm already thirty minutes late.

I round the next corner. The road takes a dip toward the lake and runs parallel to the water, though the trees hide it from view. Then a few rooftops poke through the trees, and my jaw drops when my tires bump over a narrow stone bridge and Carlton Landing spreads before me, offering adorable houses, their picturesque porches inviting with rocking chairs or dangling swings. I pass a pickleball court tucked away in the trees and a community pool perfect to laze away a warm evening.

My lousy mood vanishes.

In town, I turn past a tiny school to a restaurant called The Meeting House. And there's Ava outside on the stone patio, all radiant beside her fiancé, Hudson. Crisscrossing lines of strung lights sparkle over tables and catch the highlights in her blonde hair as she waves, jumping up and down on her toes.

Laughing, I wave back. Maybe this won't be so bad after all.

She directs me to pull off the main road and park out back. Then she cuts through the patio, trots over, and wraps me in a hug when I slide from my seat. "You made it! I'm so glad you're here."

"Of course I made it. And"—I bend into my car—"I brought your something blue."

I hold the ICEE out with both hands, and she snags it, giving me another one-armed squeeze. "You're the best."

She takes a blissful sip of the half-melted drink, then pauses and slides the straw from her lips. "Where are your shoes?" Her eyes widen. The straw comes out like a baton and points between her ICEE and my knee area. "And what happened to your skirt?"

"Oh, nothing. Let's just say the first ICEE came to an unfortunate end. The rudest boy in the world dumped it on me." I pop my trunk. "Where can I change?"

"I'm so sorry." Her shoulders slump, and a dollop of ICEE drips from her straw before she slides it back into her drink. "It's all my fault."

I rummage for a pair of jeans and some sandals. "I assure you, it's not."

She slurps another sip. "There's a bathroom inside. And don't worry. We're still waiting on one of the groomsmen. But Hudson says he's close."

While she saunters back to the patio, I run inside to swap out my clothes, wash my feet in the sink—yeah, gross—and check my makeup. Too bad I don't have time to shower after the ICEE ordeal, but this will have to do.

Back at my car, I toss my skirt in the trunk, then walk up the stone pathway to the patio where our party mingles. The welcome smell of something delicious wafts over me, and my empty stomach growls.

I greet Ava's parents, and of course, her mom comments on my tardiness while her husband is perfectly sweet. Hudson hugs me. He and Ava introduce me to everyone else: his parents and sisters, several sets of grandparents, other family members, and the wedding planner, Evelyn, one of Ava's mom's good friends, all the way from Houston.

Ava slips her arm through mine. "We're going to have a fabulous weekend. You'll love Carlton Landing, and the wedding will be amazing."

Maybe she's right.

As we claim our seats at the beautifully set table, Hudson grins, puts his fingers to his lips, and lets out an earsplitting whistle. He waves over our heads. "Will's here. Finally."

A gray car pulls into the alley, and he rushes to greet his groomsman, feet crunching across the gravel. When the newcomer emerges, I suck in a quick breath. The breeze blows a few tendrils of hair across my face, and I slap it away and blink.

No way.

Ava sidles next to me. "That's Hudson's cousin Will. Isn't he cute? And he's single too." She cocks her head. "But what is he wearing?"

Is it too late to crawl back to my car and drive home?

Of course, the late groomsman would be a gorgeous dark-haired guy wearing blue-spotted shorts and a neon-yellow, eight-dollar T-shirt that reads *Fish Eufaula*. The rudest boy in the world.

3

Will

"You found it!" My cousin Hudson—the groom at this poorly timed event—jogs over to grab me into an uncharacteristic hug. He must be all keyed up about his looming nuptials.

I can't help but smile at his enthusiasm. "Sorry I'm late."

"That's okay. Sorry you had such a long day. Besides, you're just in time. One of the bridesmaids just got here too." He offers a sly grin. "We've been wanting to introduce you two. I think you'll hit it off."

"Please don't try to set me up again. That didn't go well last time. In fact, I've sworn off the practice."

"They can't all be that bad. This one's a winner." He winks. "*And* easy on the eyes."

I shake my head. "No chance. I've had my fill of setups. Never again."

He claps me on the shoulder. "You hungry?"

"Starving. I haven't eaten since my layover in Dallas before taking off for the Tulsa airport."

Not taking his hand from my shoulder, he finally looks me over. "What's up with your shirt?"

"It's a long story."

"I was hoping you'd look a little more…cool when I introduce you to Morgan."

"It doesn't matter because I don't trust you to introduce me to anyone. And besides, what you see is what you get. Lost my luggage, remember? I don't have anything. No underwear, no toothbrush, nothing."

He chuckles. "Come on. I'll take you into town to Dollar General after dinner."

Great.

I follow him toward a group in a shaded courtyard under twinkling lights.

He pivots, walking backward, and gestures. "What'd you spill on your shorts?"

My fingers twitch to pick at the now-dry but still-sticky blue stains. "I didn't spill anything. Some psycho decided to dump an entire blue ICEE on me."

Hudson spins back around and steps aside, and the beautiful brown eyes of that very psycho—uh, girl— blink at me.

My mouth drops open before I slam it closed. Can I please hit rewind on this day?

Scowling, she crosses her arms. "Ava, did he just say some 'psycho decided' to dump ICEE on him?"

"Hey, Ava." I give the bride a little wave.

Ava gestures with her drink. Is that *the* ICEE? "Oh, please tell me this isn't the 'rudest boy in the world' from the gas station?"

Rudest boy in the world? I raise an eyebrow.

Neither of us speaks. The parents and grandparents gawk.

"Great. You've met." Ava slurps her drink, her sarcasm as caustic as those blue chemicals. "And in case you were wondering, you both have names. Morgan, Will. Will, Morgan. Ready to eat? Come on, Grandma." She hooks her arm through an older woman's, leads her toward the table, and abandons the frozen drink. Gotta be pure liquid by now.

The word *grandma* seems to draw the two of us out of our trance.

Hudson slaps our shoulders and laughs. But it falls flat when neither of us cracks a smile. "Let's let bygones be bygones, huh? It's our wedding weekend."

He's right, of course.

The girl—Morgan, is it?—gives a tight-lipped nod.

I finally offer Hudson a grin. "No problem. And no one says bygones, man. I know you're older than me, but exactly how old are you?" I loop an arm around his neck and haul him across the stone patio, treating him like he used to treat me when I was shorter and scrawnier. We've spent many a summer and Christmas vacation here. I can let it go. It will be like old times. I'll stick with him for the next two days. Have a good time. Be a good cousin and then head straight out of town the second the wedding is over on Saturday.

Hudson shakes me off. "Hey, kid, remember I'm older and wiser. Doesn't matter that you're taller than me now."

I check over my shoulder. Morgan frowns at me until Ava motions her over. Her face breaks into a smile. Man, she is easy on the eyes. Lean athletic build, long golden-brown hair, warm brown eyes, a heart-shaped smile.

If I hadn't stopped at that wretched convenience store for a wretched cup of coffee, I'd be meeting her right now, and that radiant smile would be directed at me.

Well, a raspberry ICEE and my own frustration stole that opportunity. I yelled at her, aided in ruining her shoes, and called her a psycho. Not a great first impression.

I'm an idiot.

I turn back to Hudson—time to focus.

Wedding. Groomsman. Bygones.

We meander to the table, and I find my place card. Wouldn't you know, Morgan's sitting right across from me. She's already scowling in my direction.

This should be fun.

4

Morgan

I can't believe it. Of course, at a prewedding dinner for twenty, my friend, the overorganized bride, would use place cards. And, of course, I'm sitting across from the rudest boy in the world.

Psycho! He called me psycho. My hands ball into fists in my lap.

He's been cordial since we sat down an hour ago, and during a toast, he even caught my eye to mouth, "Sorry."

Not accepted, buddy. Not. Accepted.

If he weren't also the cutest boy in the world, this would all be so much easier. I'm *not* watching him interact with his mema sitting next to him. Still, it's starting to melt my icy mood.

As a cousin to the groom, Will's related to everyone on Hudson's dad's side of the family and is chatting away.

I only know a few people here, and none of them well, except Ava. I'm the nineteenth wheel in this group, even if next to me the bride's leaning away, talking to some of her extended family. Where's Tonya, the maid of honor? She's another person I'd know from the many times I visited Ava at OU, but she's not here.

My parents and I live in Edmond, and back in the day, I loved to make the trek down to Norman to stop by Ava and Tonya's dorm. I was a middle schooler visiting my older neighbor at college. I was seriously the coolest, or that's how I saw it. And even though Ava and the others I met during those visits have all graduated and moved on, I found a love for OU. I hope to go there next year when it's my turn to run off to college.

But for now, I need to focus on not feeling awkward because I'm by far the youngest person here. Well, me and Will.

The offensive boy laughs at something his mema says.

Is it too soon to excuse myself and escape to the rental house I'm sharing with Ava and the other bridesmaids? Maybe indulge in a long shower and a comfy spot to curl up with my Kindle.

I so need a reset.

And by the looks of it, Will does too. His elbows rest on the table as he twists a thin, handmade blue-and-white braided bracelet around his wrist. He covers his mouth as he yawns, scrunching the slightly pink skin over his nose. The remnants of a sunburn? That yellow shirt lights up his tanned skin, but its radiance is a fake. He's probably too exhausted even to be rude now.

Oops, he's caught my stare. As he hides his hands—and the bracelet—under the table, I swing my head the other way.

Ava pulls me into their conversation by leaning forward and asking, "How's your summer job, Morgan? The snow cone stand, right?"

I swallow my last bit of Parmesan chicken and put my fork down. "It's good. Fine."

This is overstated since I'm not a big fan of the job or the cramped hut, to be honest. But hopefully, I've sidestepped more questions.

I'm wrong, of course.

Ava's mom, Fran, pushes salad around her plate as she practically yells down the table. "Morgan, I thought you had a job with that baker on Bryant Street, the cute little place with the pink cupcakes on the sign."

Uh-oh, with that high-pitched tone, she's probably had too much to drink.

"Mom, I told you she doesn't do that anymore."

"Oh, that's right. Well, too bad. Otherwise, Ava could've hired you to make the desserts for her bridal lunch. Or maybe even the wedding cake!"

She winks and then laughs too loudly. Apparently, the details of my exit from the culinary world are coming back to her.

My cheeks get warm. I send up a desperate prayer she won't recount the unpleasant situation.

As a server clears my plate and another places a piece of steaming blueberry pie in front of me, Ava comes to my rescue. "What's it like at Epic Ice?"

Or maybe it's not so much a rescue as a mediocre diversion since my summer job is decidedly not cool. Will's eyeing me. I shake myself. I don't care.

"It's good. Crowded in the hut during the busiest hours. But it pays pretty well, and I'm trying to save up for a study-abroad trip next summer."

"Good for you." Ava sips her tea, ice clinking in the amber liquid. "That sounds amazing. Hudson went on one of the semester-long trips. You're going to love it."

"Yeah, I can't wait."

She scoops a bite of her German chocolate cake. "Was it hard for you to get off work for the whole weekend?"

"No. Plenty of people were willing to take my shifts."

"Well, thanks for coming all this way. It means a lot."

I reassure her with a smile and grab my fork. "I wouldn't be anywhere else."

Yep, Will's still watching me. I don't look over, but maybe I should've because, once again, Fran's shouting my way.

"Morgan, are you still seeing Karen's son? He's such a darling."

I freeze, a bite of pie halfway to my mouth. Everyone is staring, including Will. I lower my fork.

"Mom!" Ava's fist tightens around her fork. "She hasn't dated Leo for months. You know that."

"Oh, right." Fran's eyes go wide. "The Haddock wedding. I heard about that. Was it only a few months ago? Seems like ages."

Ava lifts a palm toward Mr. Thompson. "Dad. Please."

Her father leans in to whisper to his wife while taking her wineglass. They erupt into a hushed argument.

I haven't moved since I heard the name Leo. I'm a statue. Maybe I'll turn into one and escape this evening. This weekend. This wedding.

The others restart their conversations, probably unsure what Fran was referring to.

"I'm so sorry." Ava touches my arm. "She can be so unaware."

Deep breath. "It's okay. She didn't know."

"She did know! Ugh. She's not allowed to drink the rest of the weekend. She's mortifying."

I force a small laugh for her sake. "It's fine." It's not. "She's right about one thing, though. It does feel like a long time ago." That may be true in some ways. In others, it feels like yesterday.

Will tilts his head, his gaze bouncing between us. Even confusion looks good on him. "What was that about?"

I catch Ava's eye, and she knows I don't want to get into it. "It all boils down to men." She pats Hudson's arm. "Some are good ones, like mine. Some aren't. The tricky part is determining who's who. They're all the same in the beginning. How can you decipher the great ones from those who are killing time until they break your heart?"

Will meets my eye, brow pinched beneath those carefree curls. Yep, he doesn't know what to say— neither do I, honestly—but when he opens his mouth to speak, Evelyn, the wedding planner, interrupts.

She's made her way to Ava. "Hey, sweetie. Can I talk to you for a moment?"

"Oh, Evelyn. You don't look so good." Ava stands.

No kidding. The wedding planner's eyes are red and puffy, and she seems short of breath.

The two of them move away for a private conversation, and several people around the table take Ava's exit as a cue to head back to their rental properties.

Maybe I can escape too. I stall over one more sip of tea.

"You know, honey." Will's mema holds up a hand beside her mouth, stage-whispering to me, then pats his hand. A dangerous mischief gleams in her eyes. "This one's actually great, one of the good ones. And it sounds like you're both single."

While she winks and sings the last part, I nearly spew tea all over the table.

Will's ears pink again. "Mema."

I try to convert my cough into a laugh as she says good night and makes her exit.

After a moment, I stand, toss my napkin on the table, and mimic Mema's exaggerated whisper. "I don't think she knows about the psycho comment."

He groans and dips his chin.

Ava returns, a tote bag hanging over her shoulder. She grips the back of a chair. By now, only Hudson, Will, and I still linger near our end of the table.

Hudson touches her arm. "You look stressed."

"Evelyn doesn't feel well. She thinks she's having some sort of allergic reaction to the allergens here. It's different from in Houston."

"Uh-oh." He squeezes her fingers.

"It's fine." She whooshes out a breath. "Everything is fine. She says she's sure she'll feel better by morning. She went on to bed."

I nod. "Of course, she will. Everything will be great."

"It turns out she's put off several tasks until the last minute. She should be able to work on most everything tomorrow, but I'm going to get my parents to help me tackle the guest favors tonight."

Hudson scoots his chair back. "I'll help."

Down the table, Ava's parents have started up another fight. This time, a bit louder. Her smile falters.

So much for curling up with my book. "I can help too. The three of us can knock it out in no time."

Ava perks up. "Oh, thank you, thank you. I don't think I can handle my parents right now. And guess what." She lifts the tote bag for Hudson, a genuine smile spreading across her lips. "I have all our matching shirts for tomorrow! You're going to love them!" She unfolds a pink one, jiggling it so the word *bride* shimmers in its gold lettering.

"Nice." Hudson doesn't manage much enthusiasm.

Not noticing, Ava throws it back in the bag and then hooks an arm through his. "There's one for everyone. Yours says 'groom,' of course." They walk away, heading toward the sidewalk. He kisses her forehead.

I catch Will's eye, and the expression on his face says, "I really doubt I'll love the shirt."

I can't help but agree.

But then our moment of agreement ends when he says, "It's going to be so weird if yours says 'psycho' and mine says 'rudest boy in the world.'"

I glare. I think my mouth drops open. Is this how it's going to be all weekend?

"Too soon?" He rubs the back of his neck. His lips quirk into a half smile. "Truce, at least?"

The word *psycho* pops into my head. "No chance."

I leave him standing there as I follow Ava out to my car, thinking about all the ways I plan to avoid him over the next three days. Shouldn't be hard.

5

Will

Twenty minutes later, Hudson and I are headed out to his truck, Ava close on our heels. "Hudson, wait. I thought you were helping."

She might've said she wasn't worried about getting everything done. But with her lips drawn and her eyebrows creased, it doesn't look like that's true.

I slide into my seat as Hudson grips her shoulders. "Relax. We'll be back in about thirty minutes, and then I'll be all in. Dollar General closes at ten. You don't want Will going without a toothbrush, right?"

"No, definitely not." She slumps and then cranes to wave at me through the passenger window. "Especially since he needs to make up with Morgan."

Before I can get a word in, Hudson hugs her, climbs into the cab, and cranks the engine. "Be back in a few."

Ava waves us off.

"You know, she's right." He adjusts the radio. "You need to make things right with Morgan. If for no other reason than I'm begging you. Ava's stressed as it is. Her parents fight every step of the way. She can't take more bickering. We're starting to wish we'd eloped."

"Your parents would kill you. And I've tried to talk to Morgan. She hates me."

"No, she doesn't. She isn't the type to hold a grudge. Also, it's not the best idea to call someone a psycho."

I throw my hands up. "I didn't know she was standing there. Or that I'd ever see her again."

"Still. Not a good idea. Ever."

I groan and rock my head back on the headrest. "I know. You're right. As always."

He chuckles. "You'd do well not to forget it."

Time to change the subject. "Does Dollar General have clothes?"

The problem with landing in Tulsa and then driving an hour and a half from the airport is I'm not likely to get my bag any time soon.

"Probably nothing you'd want to wear." Hudson makes a face. "Although it could be a step up from that shirt."

"Thanks." I smirk. "Well, I can make it until my parents get here tomorrow evening—especially since you guys provided sweet matching shirts. They're bringing a bag."

"You have to know those shirts were Ava and her mom."

"Sure. Whatever you say."

He shakes his head, and we fall into silence, listening to an old country song. I don't usually listen to country music, but somehow, it seems appropriate as we cruise along the dark, deserted highway.

Hudson powers down his window and rests his arm on it. I do the same, close my eyes, and tilt my face toward the wind whipping through my hair. It's nice being back here with him.

"So," he says, "Morgan's cute. I'm sure you noticed."

My eyelids pop open, and I groan. "What are you doing? She hates me, and I refuse to be set up ever again." As he eyes me, I relent. "And, yes, of course, I noticed."

"She doesn't hate you. And you'll hit it off if you get over yourselves. Too bad things started this way."

"Yeah, well, they did." I drum my fingers on my armrest. "What college is she going to?"

"She'll be a senior this year."

"She's in high school? She's way too young."

"Dude. She's two months younger than you. And lest we forget, you were literally in high school four weeks ago."

"Is she from Norman like Ava?"

"No, her family lives in Edmond, next door to Ava's parents."

"See. It doesn't matter how it started. It ends with us going in opposite directions after the weekend. It's pointless. I don't do long distance."

"You realize that's only a forty-minute drive from OU. You're moving in a few weeks."

"Still, no long distance. Even forty minutes. Not anymore."

"Yeah, I never talked to you about Olivia and your long-distance breakup. Sorry about her."

"You should be. It's all your fault for setting us up." I chuckle. "It's fine. I'm over it. But I'm not ready to date again." I run a hand through my hair. "Can I call *her* a psycho?"

He snorts. "Tempting. But no. Hey, are you still heading home after the wedding on Saturday? You know, we have the rental until noon on Sunday, and Mema's property is always open."

"Yeah, that's the plan. I want to make it back home for an end-of-summer pool party on Saturday night."

"That'll be a late drive."

"I'm sure I'll make it before it's over." I hold up a hand, crossing my fingers. "And hopefully before Scarlet leaves."

"Will, that girl's been off-and-on stringing you along since freshman year."

"Ouch." He's not wrong. "But I have a good feeling about this last get-together before we both head off to OU."

"Well, you can stay if you want." He shoots me a sideways glance. "Morgan is."

I groan, shift in my seat, and tip my face to the breeze again. The moon shines bright in the Oklahoma sky.

"Fine." He cuffs my shoulder. "I'll leave it alone. For now. But could you at least try to get along with her?"

"Maybe. Can you at least try not to set me up this weekend?"

We pull in under glowing yellow lights, and he puts the truck in park. Neither of us verbally agrees to the other's request, though, for his sake, I'll do my best.

We slide from the cab, and as Hudson slams his door, he shrugs. "Well, for now, let's focus on your hygiene. And perhaps how scratchy these Dollar General underwear will be."

Awesome.

6

Morgan

I'm sprawled out on a stylish gray couch, munching on microwave popcorn, and filling tiny clear plastic jars with personalized chocolates, when Ava straightens, tightening the band around her blonde ponytail.

"So, what do you think of Hudson's cousin?"

Something in me that was very near to falling asleep jumps to attention. "You mean besides the psycho comment?"

"Ah, there you are. I was wondering if you were awake."

I smirk. "I'm not superhuman. I got up early to pack, stood on my feet at Epic Ice all afternoon, and then drove all the way here."

For the past half hour, Ava's been sitting on the whitewashed hardwood floor, chattering away about the weekend schedule. We set to work after she led me on a tour of our house, an adorable three-bedroom rental called The Blue Moon. Her excited voice needed no interjection from me and was beginning to lull me to sleep.

I throw ribbon scraps at her—which flutter straight to the ocean-blue rug—and then sit up. "If I'm being honest, I stopped listening after I heard the word *spa.*"

She laughs and throws her pile of scraps at me. They also flutter to the floor. It's supposed to be a surprise, but Tonya, the maid of honor, has arranged massages for all the ladies tomorrow. I can't wait.

"Well?"

"Well, what?"

"What do you think of Will? He's cute, right?"

"I'm excited about the spa because I'll hardly have to see him tomorrow." Hopefully, it will take hours.

Her smile falters. Oops, time to appease her. "Just kidding. I'm sure he's fine."

She stands and moves to the kitchen. Boxes of wedding things clutter the table under a modern farmhouse-style light fixture. "He's a nice guy. I got to know him over the holidays when I came up with Hudson. Their whole family comes here for Christmas every year." She rips open another box of jars and begins arranging them in neat rows on the table. "They have a huge family. Nine cousins in all, I think. But Will's the only other male."

I scoop up the ribbon scraps. "That's a lot of girls."

"Yeah, the girls used to make Hudson and Will serve them at their tea parties. They hated it, but they agreed so the girls would play cops and robbers later."

I laugh, enjoying the thought of Will's cousins bossing him around.

"Do they all live in the Tulsa area?"

"No, most of them live closer to Oklahoma City." She drops into a loopback chair, a corner of her mouth turning up. "You should give him a chance."

"He called me a psycho and yelled at me at the gas station. Isn't that a red flag or something?"

"That is unfortunate. Stupid boy. Did you yell back?"

"Well, yeah. I had to defend myself."

"Two wrongs don't make a right. Do I need to quote a Bible verse about forgiveness?"

I roll my eyes. No, I already know them. "I can forgive him—*eventually*—but that doesn't mean I want to date him. Besides, after the Leo incident, I swore off dating until college, and I'm sticking to it. Hopefully, in that time, I'll decide boys aren't all pushy and rude."

"What if Leo came running back to you? You'd take him back, wouldn't you?"

"What? No. No way." His beautiful face pops into my mind. Things were so great in the beginning, but I wouldn't take him back. Would I?

She shrugs and rummages in a box, but that twist of her mouth says what she doesn't. Great, she doesn't quite believe me. "Well, either way, it's time to move on, and Will's so cute and sweet."

"I can agree he's cute."

"Who's cute?" a male voice says from the hallway just before the screen door snaps shut. Hudson walks in and then lowers his voice, glancing over his shoulder. "Are you guys talking about Will?"

"Yes," Ava says at the same time I say, "No."

Hudson slides onto a barstool. "He's taking his bags in next door."

Ava throws an arm around his neck, and they both observe me as if I'm a fun science experiment. "She thinks he's cute. It's a good start."

Hudson nods and tosses some popcorn in his mouth. "We can work with that."

"Please don't," I moan. "Can't we just focus on your wedding?"

"Sure. Sure. But you should know we're good at multitasking."

The screen door snaps again. Ava wags her eyebrows.

"In here." Hudson gives me a wink.

They're mortifying. So much for avoiding the most annoying boy in the world. Guess I'll have to shift to ignoring.

Will walks in, all nervous and windblown...and cute.

Dang it. This might be more difficult than I thought.

7

Will

Well, if I thought Morgan was going to warm up to me, I was wrong. She's hardly said a word, and she hasn't glanced in my direction. How do you play nice with a girl who won't look at you?

Hudson keeps glaring at me like it's my fault.

Can we please finish this task so I can go to bed? I'm exhausted.

A few minutes ago, Morgan got up to go to the bathroom, and in her absence, Hudson and Ava laid into me.

"What are you doing?"

"Have you apologized?"

"Why are you being weird?"

"I'm not being weird! She's ignoring me." I fumble another ribbon into a passable bow. "And let me remind you—I'm not interested in a setup."

What I'm interested in is going to bed. Instead, I'm sitting on a blue rug and using the coffee table as my workspace, and Morgan is, of course, sitting as far away as possible at the kitchen table.

"You're not trying. Forget the setup. Just act like normal humans."

"I am trying. You guys aren't helping, making it all awkward. And maybe I don't want to talk to *her*."

Hudson starts to say something else, but Ava's phone rings. She steps outside to take the call as footsteps scuffle overhead. Morgan makes her way downstairs and back to her spot.

And shocker, Hudson takes the opportunity to get something from the fridge.

Morgan and I work in silence.

"So," I say, and "how 'bout that weather" pops into my head. I have enough brainpower left to hold it in.

She raises a brow.

Say something. Anything. "Are you excited for your senior year?"

She dips her head over the tiny bow she's tying. It unravels, and she sighs. "Yeah, I guess. Should be fun."

I finish another chocolate jar and toss it into the box. "Need some help with that?"

She snorts. "I don't need your help."

Ava emerges from the porch and pauses at the door. A tear leaks from a red-rimmed eye. Uh-oh.

I stand, and Morgan launches from her chair, rushing to Ava's side. "Are you okay? What's wrong?"

Hudson comes back in and wraps her in a hug. "What's up, babe?"

"Mom is impossible. Why does she make everything so difficult? She called to complain about the florist and to tell me the bakery where we ordered cookies for brunch on Saturday canceled the order. I mean, that's not a big deal. Couldn't she keep it to herself?" She waves toward the jars and ribbons strewn across the table. "And why oh why didn't she let me use one of the local wedding planners here? They have a full service. But, no, Mom insisted we use Evelyn. This stuff should have been done ages ago. I thought it *was* done."

Hudson rubs her back. "Hey, everything will be okay."

"Mom was going to tell me something else, but she must've sensed I was losing it. So she refused to tell me." Arms around his waist, she snuggles in to Hudson. "Is everything falling apart? What else is going to go wrong? Cookies, rude flower shops, mystery emergency." She points between Morgan and me. "And these two won't even *try* to get along."

Another tear races down her cheek. Great. I'm the worst kind of idiot.

Morgan and I eye each other. Some mutual agreement forms.

She places a hand on Ava's arm. "We can get along. We promise. Right, Will?"

"Yeah, no problem."

Hudson spends the next minutes consoling Ava, and when she retreats upstairs, he spreads his hands at us. "Okay, that's it, you two. Either play nice or pretend to. Got it."

We nod.

"Good." He picks up a box of jars and scoops all the unfinished ones into it. "These need to go back to Evelyn. She said she'll deal with them tomorrow when she feels better, and hopefully, she can finish them off. There's only half a box left, but we're all too tired and emotional. Think you two can manage to walk these over there without fighting while I tell Ava good night?"

We nod again.

"Okay, then."

I take the box. He blurts a quick set of directions, and Morgan grabs the other.

As we descend the front porch steps, the nighttime sounds of crickets, frogs, and locusts surround us. We walk down the boardwalk until it gives way to the paved sidewalk.

Finally, she breaks the silence. "He's right. We need to get along."

The soft glow of strung lights on the house we're passing reflects in her eyes. Ducking my head before she can catch me staring, I clear my throat. "Agreed." I shift the box to one arm and stick my hand out. "Truce?"

She rolls her eyes and tries to do the same, but the box tips and half the plastic jars fall to the sidewalk and bounce every which way. "Oh no!" She rights the box, and I laugh and drop to pick them up.

When she scowls, I try to wipe the smile from my face.

"It's not funny! What if they'd shattered?"

"They didn't. Look. Plastic." I hold one up, and she squats next to me and swipes another.

"There's dirt on this one."

"Wipe it off. They'll never know. It's fine."

We gather them up, and when we stand and meet each other's eyes, she gives me another look, her brow pinched. "What?"

The top of her head meets the height of my chin. She smells like coconut and fresh flowers. I'm trying to hide another smile. "Nothing. Just laughing at the fact that things get messy when we're together. ICEE. Wedding favors. What's next?"

"Right. The ICEE incident. I'd almost forgotten. Thanks for reminding me."

She shifts away from me and keeps walking.

She's cute when she's mad. Fighting another smile, I jog to catch up. "Hey, truce, remember?"

"I remember. I'll be all sunshiny when we're with Ava and Hudson. They'll never know how much I loathe you." Maybe, that's a hint of a smile.

"Your loathing will be our little secret."

And just when things are starting to improve, we turn the corner onto Redbud Street and are met with flashing lights.

Morgan pauses and then picks up the pace. "That's not good."

Nope. I follow, hustling toward the ambulance in the driveway of the very house we're heading to.

No, not good at all.

8

Morgan

Fran's frantic voice emerges before her. When the front door bursts open, she and a stretcher spill out onto the porch.

Oh boy.

Her thin frame props the door as two paramedics wheel the wedding planner out and down the front porch steps.

"Oh, this is so ill-timed." Clearly in a panic, she lets the door fall closed. "We need you. What are we going to do?"

She traipses after them across the grass in her spiked heels. Evelyn lies on the stretcher and glares at Fran over her oxygen mask. She says nothing.

"Wow, she is the worst."

"She really is." Great. Did I just agree with Will? Ignore that. I rush toward the insufferable woman. "What happened?"

"Oh, Morgan." She waves over her head, breathing heavily. "What are we going to do? How will we survive the weekend without her? She's just going to leave."

Seriously? "She's leaving on a stretcher. Is she okay?" Evelyn's eyes are open, and the paramedics seem calm, so we're not dealing with anything life-threatening. Right?

"Heavens, I hope so. Something to do with asthma and severe allergies." She flaps her arms, then crosses them, and taps her lips with one finger. "Maybe she'll be better tomorrow. Maybe she can come back. I have to go tell Bob." She starts to trot away, then pivots back. "You cannot tell Hudson and Ava. We'll figure it out. They don't need to know."

The paramedics are loading the stretcher. A few neighbors have come out to see what's going on. I lift my palms. "Mrs. Thompson, they're going to find out."

"Eventually. But by then, I'll have a plan B." She puts a hand on each of our shoulders. "Promise me you won't tell them."

I hesitate, then nod. Will does too.

"Good." She pats us each on the cheek. "Oh, what are we going to do?" She rushes away, trying to run up the hill in her ridiculous shoes.

Will's eyebrows are so high they're practically lost in his shaggy hair. Red and blue lights flash over his face. "Whoa."

"Yeah. She's a lot."

"Hey, kid." One of the paramedics motions us over. "Where'd that lady go?"

"I'm not sure. That way?"

"Seriously?" He rolls his eyes and slams the ambulance's back door.

It pulls away and rounds the next corner. The lights fade into the distance. The neighbors go back into their houses.

I let out a breath and brush a strand of hair from my face. "What just happened?"

Will shifts the box he's holding. "I'm not sure, but I feel like an accomplice to a crime."

"Should we keep this a secret?"

"Maybe. Until tomorrow. You saw Ava tonight."

"Okay." I jostle my box. "Well, we can't go back with these."

"Right." He moves toward the front porch.

I follow. "What are you doing?"

"Maybe they left the door unlocked."

Sure enough, we push the door open and walk right in. It wasn't even latched.

"Hudson told me all the rental houses for the wedding party are booked through the weekend. We can drop these boxes here. Tomorrow, when the maid of honor gets here, she can deal with what this means."

"Good plan."

The corner of his mouth lifts. "Hey, we agreed on something."

No comment.

We cross the rug into the living room. Boxes are stacked on the coffee table, side chairs, and in front of the fireplace. We add ours. Several lids stand open. Golden pieces from some sort of decoration lay disassembled in a heap.

I open another box. Same thing. Oh my.

Will catches my frown. "What's wrong?"

"I get the feeling there are a lot of things left to do." I hover over the mess. "Everything in that box is supposed to be part of the reception centerpieces. They're not even assembled."

He jams his hands on his hips. "We need to pretend we didn't see this."

"I wonder if Fran noticed."

He shrugs and picks up a yellow notepad from the coffee table. "Look at this."

"Is that a list of tasks?"

"Seems to be." He flips the page to more items. "Only about half of these are checked off."

"Oh man. What do we do?"

He flops the notepad back on the coffee table. Dark circles rim his eyes, and his shoulders slump. The excitement of seeing an ambulance has worn off. "Well, seeing as it's after midnight and we have to be at the coffee shop at nine, we save this mess for tomorrow. Maybe Fran will have an awesome plan B."

"Right." I purse my lips. What's Ava going to think of all this? Her big moment is less than forty-eight hours away. This weekend's gotta be great for her.

We don't find any keys, but we turn off the lights and close the front door before heading back down the hill toward the boardwalk.

I straighten my shoulders, hoping for the best. "It's going to be fine. They'll figure it out."

Will yawns. "Yeah. Tomorrow's a new day. We can get back to ignoring each other in private and pretending to get along in public. It'll be great."

"Of course." I tear my gaze from his. I don't like him and need to stop being mesmerized by his dark eyes. He called me psycho! "For the record, I'm still mad at you."

"Figured."

Warmth infuses the word, and he doesn't seem the least bit concerned. Somehow, this, plus his stupid shirt and stupid pretty eyes, infuriates me. I don't even say bye when I veer off and up the steps to The Blue Moon.

He laughs behind me as I pull the door open. "Good night, Morgan."

I shut the door and flip the deadbolt, locking him out of the house and out of my mind.

Well, at least one of those things is possible.

9

Will

I walk into Coffee Connection, and the aroma hits me like a cozy bolt of lightning. Man, I need it. Desperately. I'm rolling in on way too little sleep.

Clinking dishes and jittery chatter further enliven the air. Almost everyone in the tiny coffee shop—including me—is wearing matching pink or green T-shirts stamped with glittery words *bridesmaid, father of the groom, flower girl,* etc. We make an absurd group, like overgrown kindergarteners on a field trip.

Clearly, this groomsman isn't fit to talk to anyone until I'm caffeinated, so I order a latte from the barista, a cute girl about my age, and have a seat on a polished stool at the coffee bar. No one is freaking out about the wedding planner. Fran must've kept her secret.

I hide my ruined tennis shoes under my stool as I scratch at a faint stain on my khaki shorts. The blue remnants didn't quite come out when I washed them in the sink last night. Sadly, Dollar General had no shorts in my size except for a pair of too-short, fishing-themed swim trunks. I bought them. But only for emergencies. At least my parents will be here this afternoon.

I pull my phone from my pocket. Mema catches my eye and gives me a wave from a table with my cousin Emma and her parents. I wave back. Ava and Hudson are deep in conversation with Hudson's parents while other family members and friends mill about, catching up and laughing. No Morgan.

I swing back around and make the mistake of opening Instagram. Photos of my high school buddies still having fun on our senior trip fill my feed. They mock me with their happy smiles as they pose on the sandy beach. The ocean spreads behind them. Disgusted, I consider shoving it back in my pocket, but I'm a glutton for punishment. My thumb keeps pushing new photos onto the screen as I try to remind myself that I'll see them on Saturday night at the pool party when they're home and all this wedding business is behind me.

A ding sounds as the door swings open, and I glance over my shoulder. Morgan walks in. All sleepy-eyed and smiles, she greets others around the room. Huh, maybe it's just me, but that pink bridesmaid shirt doesn't seem so bad on her.

She directs that smile at Mema when she passes her table, and Mema says something I can't quite hear. Morgan giggles and then yawns, and I'm left dying to know what Mema said.

Morgan mumbles about getting coffee when Ava, perky as ever, tries to wave her to their table next. As Morgan frowns at me, a tinge of disappointment pinches my chest. Doesn't seem much changed overnight.

But I'm in her path to coffee, so she has no choice but to join me at the coffee bar. She tries to snag the barista's attention, and if I'm not mistaken, the girl is ignoring her. Ha. Good.

"Nice shirt," I say after a beat.

"Thanks." She doesn't crack a smile. "But what's up with yours? You look ridiculous."

The barista places a mug in front of me with a wink. I smile back, aware Morgan is watching us. The girl walks away, not taking Morgan's order.

There's a heart shape in the foam.

Morgan peers at the heart. When she raises her head, giving me a full view of her alluring dark eyes now all aglow, she lifts a brow. Without breaking a smile or taking her gaze off me, she grabs the little spoon next to the mug and stirs the heart away as I try to keep from grinning.

"That's better," she says. "Should I tell her to be careful? You do tend to spill your coffee all over people."

"Oh, are we joking about that now?"

Her lips form a thin line. The word *psycho* must be floating around in her head. "Definitely not."

Another barista takes her coffee order, and within a minute, he sets a mug of black coffee in front of her.

"Need any half-and-half for that?"

She pulls it close with a contented sigh. "No thanks."

When the barista walks away, I lean over her mug. "Perfect. Black like your unforgiving heart."

She lets her lips curve into a hint of a smile. Wow, I like making her smile. But I don't want to like it. All the reasons I shouldn't get involved with her still stand. Plus, she still hates me. Maybe.

She takes a sip. "If I have a black heart, it's because a boy made it that way. I don't trust your kind."

"My kind, as in men in general."

She shakes her head. "Boys in general."

I smirk. "Sounds like there's a story there."

"Maybe. But I'm not telling you." She places her mug back on the counter and taps my phone where it lies on the counter. "Dreaming about the beach? You know there's one here?"

I dim the screen and hide the phone in my pocket. "Yes. Actually, I had to leave my senior trip early to be here. I was torturing myself by looking at the photos."

"Oh." She wraps her fingers around the mug. "That sucks. And explains the sunburn."

"Yeah."

I touch my nose and then take another sip of coffee, not hating her sympathetic look. I lift a shoulder. "It's fine. And I'd hardly consider a manufactured lake beach comparable to the Florida coast."

"Fair point, but Ava said the one here is pretty cute. I haven't been down there yet."

"No? You should. And she's right. It's not bad." I'm just bitter. FOMO is real.

Before I can say something stupid like "maybe I could show you," she inches closer to whisper. "Have you heard anything about Evelyn?"

Fran seems to be ignoring us. If I'm not mistaken, the words *mother of the bride* are printed in a larger, fancier font than on anyone else's shirt. I pitch my voice low. "Not a word. I guess she was serious about not telling anyone."

"I hope she's okay."

"Yeah, me too. Maybe someone will check on her today."

"Hopefully, but who knows? I doubt Fran'll think of it."

"She's the worst."

"She really is. I don't like sharing a secret with her. But I bet it's not long until people start to notice the wedding planner has disappeared." She swings her stool around, facing the other direction. "Tonya and Matt arrived this morning."

Yeah, the matron of honor stands next to her husband near the self-serve station. "I don't think she knows Fran's secret, either. Do you know Tonya?"

"She was Ava's college roommate. I've met her several times."

Noticing our attention, Tonya cracks a smile and glides our way. She pulls Morgan into a hug. "Wow, you look so grown up. I can't believe how long it's been since I've seen you. How's life?"

"Good. How are you and Matt?"

"We're great." She taps my arm and lowers her voice to sultry tones. "And who's your friend?"

I'm pretty sure she already knows.

Morgan clears her throat. "This is Will, one of the groomsmen."

Yeah, like my shirt wouldn't clue her in.

"Hey, Will. You two are getting chummy over here, whispering away. I guess things are going well?" She winks at Morgan as if I'm not sitting here and then leans in to whisper in Morgan's ear. "Ava was right. You look great together."

Morgan's mouth drops open, and I pretend I didn't hear.

Just when Morgan seems on the verge of responding, Tonya spins around. "Okay, everyone, listen up!" She claps. "We've got an awesome day planned for you!"

Morgan's cheeks are the color of a cherry-flavored ICEE.

I laugh, lowering my voice. "It's because we have matching shirts. Of course, we look good together."

This doesn't seem to soften her mood as she twirls strands of that long dark hair around a finger.

Tonya's husband, Matt, stands. "Our day is going to start with"—he rubs his hands together—"a cruise on the lake in our friends' party barge!"

An excited murmur erupts, and even I'm optimistic. I haven't been out on a boat in ages. Will there be tubing? Wakeboarding?

Matt scoops up a clipboard. "And later this afternoon, we're organizing a bocce ball tournament for the guys."

"And, ladies." Tonya flips her red curls over her shoulder, then winks at Ava. "We'll be at the spa for facials and massages."

"Things are looking up. Lake time in the morning." I rub my hands together like Hudson did. "And we don't even have to be around each other this afternoon."

Morgan grins, then salutes me with her mug. "Excellent point. This is going to be a great day."

Mrs. Thompson, still wearing spiked high heels, claims the audience. "Sounds amazing, Tonya. How lovely. Now, everyone, let's hop on outside, snap a photo, and then finish our bagels on the boat."

She starts ushering everyone out, but before Morgan and I get a chance to step toward the door, Fran pulls Morgan aside, her thin frame rigid. Curious, I hang back.

"Listen, Morgan, I—we—need you to work on a few things today." She holds out the wedding checklist she must have swiped from Evelyn's house and puts on a sorrowful expression. "Do you think you can do that for Ava? You'll have to skip the family activities today, but we would sure appreciate it."

Morgan's mouth is agape. As hurt wells up in her eyes, I can't blame her. "Um, well, I guess I could help a bit. For Ava."

"Oh, honey, you're so sweet. I knew you'd come through." Fran shoves the list into Morgan's hand. "I mean, it makes sense since these are family activities, and you're the only one who's not family. Well, besides Tonya and Matt, of course. But they planned the day."

Wow. Just wow. I cannot believe this woman. My hands ball into fists.

Morgan unrolls the list. "Which one would you like me to do?"

"Oh, all of them, really. Just start at the top and work your way down. The rest of us will just be so busy."

Morgan's shoulders slump. "Okay."

At a sudden surge of protectiveness, I consider telling Fran off, but it wouldn't get through to her pea-sized brain. And Morgan would volunteer anyway, for Ava's sake.

So, before I can stop it, my mouth opens, and I hear myself say, "I'll help her."

Morgan's frown is the inverse of Fran's smile.

What did I just do?

10

Morgan

I'm still scowling when Fran claps. "Perfect! You two will handle it so easily." She lowers her voice conspiratorially. "But no playing around now. We don't want you two getting distracted."

She winks, and my cheeks burn. Again.

Her face lights up even further. "Oh, it's perfect!" She taps a finger on her lips. "I'll use your budding romance as an excuse for why you're not with us today."

Budding romance?

I start to protest, but she plunges on. "I'll tell Ava you two volunteered to help me with a special surprise, but I think you just wanted to sneak in some alone time to get to know each other better." She claps again. "Ava's been so distracted since Tonya arrived she might not even notice you're gone."

I frown. That comment stings. Luckily, Will looks as angry and embarrassed as I am.

I clear my throat as Fran starts to turn away. "Mrs. Thompson, this is not a good idea. That's a long list, and Ava's going to find out. Besides, Will and I barely get along. We might kill each other."

She waves as if to shoo the thought away. "Oh, nonsense. You'll do great."

Oblivious to the fact that she's just embarrassed, insulted, and angered us, she reaches for the door handle. "And if you could hurry things along, that would be great too. We're counting on you two now!" She opens the door with a soft ding and joins the others on the patio.

The quaint shop is quiet after the exit of her voluminous personality.

Will lowers his head and pinches the bridge of his nose.

I shift my weight and cross my arms. "Why did you do that? Now we have to spend the whole day together."

His gaze snaps up to mine, the muscles in his jaw hardening. "I was trying to help you. Maybe do the right thing? Did you see how long that list is?"

I clench the yellow notepad. It is a long list. As it is, it will take two people an eternity to complete it, much less one person. I release a growl and scowl at the ceiling. *Lord, give me patience.* "Well, I guess we're stuck together for now."

He snatches the list. "Yep. Lucky me."

"Hey! Give that back."

See. This right here. This is why I've sworn off dating for senior year. Boys are pushy. Always trying to take over. Just like Leo did. Just like they all do.

Will walks back to his perch at the coffee bar. "Let's have another coffee and put it on the wicked witch's tab. We can get organized and decide what to do first."

"Fine." I can get behind a plan that involves more coffee. I sit on the stool next to him, snatch the paper, and put it between us. "But just so we're clear. I'm in charge."

He clenches his mug still resting on the counter, knuckles whitening. "Fine. If you want to be Fran's number-one minion, fine with me." He reads off the first few items before I can reply to his ridiculous, though not entirely off base, statement. "Assemble the archway for the florist, set up chairs for the rehearsal dinner, string lights in the pavilion, organize the—"

He trails off when I put my forehead on the bar. He folds the paper. "You're right. Too much to take in right now. Want to just start at the top?"

"I guess," I say, not lifting my head. "The archway?"

"Yeah. It shouldn't be too hard."

Right.

After we finish our first cups of coffee, the barista, who can't stop flirting with Will or glaring at me, makes us a second set to go. I shove the list into my pocket, and we emerge into the warm sunlight.

The rest of the wedding party is gone—I guess they took the photo without us. We veer left onto the sidewalk lining Water Street. A breeze teases my hair and carries scents from blooming flowers, and I take a deep breath. Kids race by on bikes, oblivious to anything other than their destination.

We follow the sidewalk, and the lake comes into view. Its surface ripples. An open grassy area slopes down to steps leading to the beach area nestled within a U-shaped rock formation. Parents and children are already out on the sand.

"You're right." I pin my hair down with a hand. "It's pretty cute."

"Yeah. I used to love coming here. Hudson and I would build sandcastles and try to catch fish with our bare hands."

My lips almost start to turn up, but they fall flat when a party barge putts within the no-wake zone. Our friends' laughter carries up the hill until someone cranks up the music, and everyone onboard sings along.

I'm a little kid again, watching the older kids ride away on their bikes for some adventure to which I wasn't invited.

Will rakes a hand through his glossy curls. "They have a tube."

We're statues as they exit the no-wake zone and the engine roars. They surge across the water, around the bend, and out of sight.

No tubing for us. No skiing. No lying out on the boat. Only work.

His hands drop to his sides. "Well, that was heartbreaking."

Why in the world did he volunteer? Guilt twinges before I squash it. He made his choice. "You could have been out there. No one asked you to stay."

He glares at me. "You're a delight. You know that?"

Ugh. This day is the worst. I cross my arms and scowl at the beach. Maybe it's not that cute after all.

A young girl grabs a handful of sand and chunks it at a boy.

Will points. "Oh, look. Is that what you were like as a child? Terrorizing boys with words and sand."

"You're mistaken. The boy's misusing his words. And oh, look"—I repeat his phrase—"he's yelling at her now because he has sand all over his shorts. Definitely you as a child."

I stalk away. Will he follow?

Why oh why, does an annoying surge of relief loosen my spine and wobble my legs when his footsteps crunch behind?

11

Morgan

As Will trails me back up the hill past porch after porch, Evelyn's rental house beckons through the trees, its sleek glass windows and sharp, angular design something off both an architectural website and a country-living blog. The lush landscaping surrounding the front porch, blooming with vibrant flowers, add pops to an otherwise neutral palette.

"Wow." I breathe deeply. "It looks so different in the daylight. These houses are gorgeous."

"Right?" Will shades his dark eyes. "It's like we're in a modern country alternate reality out here. Maybe that's why people love it so much."

"Including your family?"

"Especially my family." He clomps up the steps ahead of me. "I hope Fran didn't lock the door."

"I doubt it. She's not that responsible." And sure enough, when I try the handle, it swings open.

"I was hoping we couldn't get in." He shakes back his tousled curls. "Then we could go hang out at the pool."

I don't miss that he says *we*, but I ignore it and step into a living room as stylish as the outside, filled with modern furniture and bold artwork. Funny how I didn't notice any of this last night with everything going on.

My phone chimes as I trudge up the stairs to search the bedrooms.

Ava: Mom says you're with Will, working on a surprise. *Heart shape* I hope she didn't manipulate you into helping Evelyn. I never know with her.

Not sure how to respond, I plop down on the top step and rest my elbows on my knees. I want to tell her the truth. *Evelyn's gone, and your mom is the worst. Oh, and there's no surprise.* If I tell her, she'll come right back here and skip all the fun activities planned for her. She'll see the long list. She'll be mad at her mom. And her stress level will shoot through the roof.

I can't tell her.

Me: I'm sworn to secrecy. No questions!

There. Not a lie.

Ava: Okay. Keep your secrets. But have fun with Will. Perfect opportunity to get to know each other! *Kissy face* *Winky face*

I can't keep myself from responding to that.

Me: I may be on a secret mission for my favorite ex-neighbor, but I'm still not dating right now. Give it up. *Kissy face*

Ava: Okay, okay. But don't let your bad experience with Leo keep you from noticing someone who's actually great. And, no, all boys are NOT idiots.

Next, she sends a selfie of Hudson and her on the boat.

Me: *eye roll* Yeah, yeah, you two are precious. Have fun!

Ava sends a video meme of someone wiping out on a tube, and I laugh.

"Found it!" Will shouts from downstairs.

I rise and shove my phone in my pocket and meet him at the door leading to the garage.

He presses the opener, and an angular ray of sunlight creeps across the floor as the garage door lifts. A giant box occupies the space where a car might go. It's already been opened, and gold metal pieces spill over, some even strewn on the floor. What a mess.

"Oh man," Will mutters. "How are we supposed to get that thing to the church?"

Great question.

He nods toward the corner, curls flopping over his forehead. "Maybe we can borrow the golf cart. I'm sure Evelyn included it in her rental agreement so she could cart everything down the hill."

I run a hand over the shiny blue paint job. This brand-new vehicle boasts leather seats and an OKC Thunder basketball logo across the front.

We locate the key next to the welcome pack and, after an awkward lifting job, balance the box on the back seat. Improvising, we strip two bathrobes of their ties and use them to secure it to the cart.

At the last second, I grab the two boxes of wedding favors and stow them between us in front. Might as well load up.

We head down the hill at turtle speed. The bright midmorning sun casts shadows through the trees.

"So." Will drums his fingers on the steering wheel. "What's your last name?"

I blink, caught off guard. Given how much we enjoy each other's company, I assumed we'd ride along in stony silence.

"Whitney." I start to leave it at that. But that would be rude, and I'm totally against people being the rudest in the world. "And what's yours?"

"Jameson."

Across the street, a dad and son are playing bocce ball on one of the three narrow courts. They stare as we pass, probably wondering why two teenagers with coordinating T-shirts are carting a giant box of gold down the hill.

Will waves, and they wave back. His hands back at ten and two, he faces the wind, letting it tousle his curls. "Well, Morgan Whitney, what do you like to do for fun?"

So we're doing this. We're chitchatting. I release a sigh. "Oh, you know. Reading. Hanging out with friends. Baking sometimes. But I don't do that anymore." Why did I bring up baking? "And you?"

"I like reading too. And baseball. Paddleboarding's my latest obsession."

"As in stand-up paddleboarding?" I make a face. "I'm not sure I have enough balance for that."

"It's not hard. You should try it."

"Not likely."

"I have my board here. And Hudson has his. You might like it."

"Not going to happen."

"Your loss." Rather than push, he spins the basketball key chain hanging from the dash. "What do you like to read?"

"Lots of stuff. Contemporary. Fantasy. Historical. Romance. I don't read much nonfiction, though."

"Me either. Do you like e-books or physical books better?"

"Physical books, for sure. But I like my Kindle books too. What about you?"

"Physical book, mostly, and I like science fiction the best."

What? A book nerd? "I didn't peg you as a sci-fi fan." I grind my teeth together. And why is it attractive? Ugh.

"Hey, inside this dreamy exterior"—he indicates himself and his *groomsman* T-shirt with a circular wave of his hand—"lives a hard-core sci-fi nerd."

I roll my eyes. "I should have known."

"My cousin Emma self-published a contemporary romance. You might like it. She's here, actually. She was sitting with Mema at the coffee shop this morning."

"I didn't notice." All I noticed after noticing him was, well, him. "But I'd love to meet her and read her book."

"Her pen name is Emmie Blackwell. I'll introduce you when they get back."

I pull out my phone to look her up as he continues.

"My grandparents host a huge family Christmas here every year. Me, Emma, Hudson, and all the cousins come in during the break. We play tons of board games and hang out in that hot tub." He points at the giant hot tub next to the community pool we're passing. "Walking down here and getting in is always fun, but walking back, wet, in December is the worst." He laughs, messing with the radio but finding only static. "And even as young kids, we ran around this place in the summers like we owned it. Mom and Dad had no idea where I was half the time. And as long as I stayed with Hudson, they didn't care."

At his wistfulness, I even wish I had similar memories. "It sounds nice. I don't have many lake memories. It just isn't something we did. A friend from school invited me on their boat once. That's about the extent of my lake time."

"You're missing out. Maybe Ava will invite you some time. I'm sure she'll be here more often now that she's becoming part of the family."

"Yeah, maybe." Would Will be here too? Not that I care.

"So why don't you bake anymore?"

Hair slaps my cheek as I whip my gaze in his direction. I tuck my hair back. Oh, why did I bring that up?

His eyes are forward. But he frowns, and his shoulders inch up. "What? Did I say something wrong? Again?"

"No. It's okay. I used to love baking. And I was good at it. It's what I wanted to do someday—you know? Own a bakery. But then I had a bad experience, and now I don't bake anymore."

"A bad experience? How's that? Like you accidentally poisoned everyone at a birthday party?"

I smirk as we hit a bump. Then I reach back to wrap an arm over the box. "No. Nothing quite so drastic."

And it was more than baking. It was that horrible wedding and everyone staring. It was my mortification and public heartbreak.

Will drums his fingers again. "Your house got robbed, and someone held you at gunpoint until you gave up all your measuring spoons?"

"I'm not dignifying that with a response."

He tilts his head.

"You tried bathing in icing, and now you can't stand the smell of it."

I raise an eyebrow.

"No?" He grins. "How about, in a moment of poor judgment, you called your sous-chef—that's not the right word. Assistant baker?—a psycho?"

Seriously?

I let my smile slip, and he schools his features. "Still not ready to joke about it?"

"Nope. It's only been like an hour since the last time you asked."

He huffs. "Fine."

We pass The Meeting House, and our easy conversation dies. Was it only last night that I met this boy on that patio?

He's gone quiet. He's cute. I'll give him that. But he called me a name behind my back.

I turn my face away, pretending to study the empty sand volleyball court. Time to think about something else—anything other than the cute but annoying boy next to me.

My phone chimes in my pocket, and I pull it free, then nearly drop it when the screen displays a message from Leo. The first in a long, long time.

Leo: Can we talk?

Not exactly the distraction I had in mind. I shove it back in my pocket.

Now, I have two things to keep off my mind. Super.

12

Morgan

Driving parallel to the water, we finally approach the charming church nestled in the woods between the road and the lake. Built of stylish white siding and a silver metal roof, its dark accents create a stark contrast, a beautiful blend of small-town charm and sleek modern lines.

Will rolls over the sidewalk, and I tighten my grip on the box.

We park at the front door and begin the daunting task of unloading.

Grunting under the weight, he mutters, "How do I get myself into these things?"

I shift my hands to find a better grip. "Well—you volunteered."

"Right."

Maneuvering the box to the front door proves difficult. I'm glad he's here. This would've been impossible for one person. I'm sure he's noticed.

"Will?"

"Yeah?"

"Thanks for helping."

We lock gazes, and after a moment, he relaxes. "Sure."

We crouch side by side and drag the box through the doorway and to the front of the sanctuary. I stand and stretch out my shoulders. "This is cute."

"Yeah, when we're in town on the weekends, we attend Sunday morning worship. I like the music."

We meander around, admiring the clean lines, the stark white shiplap, and the minimalist decor. I pause by the floor-to-ceiling window stretching along the back wall and take in a breathtaking lake view.

I reach out to touch the glass but drop my hand before making contact. "At first, I wondered why Ava and Hudson decided on a church wedding when there are so many great outdoor spaces, but this is beautiful."

Will stops next to me, our shoulders almost touching. Two ducks land on the water, sending ripples toward the shore. A smile crosses my lips.

When I turn, Will's watching me. He lifts a corner of his mouth, and my cheeks warm. I'm not quite sure why.

Squaring my shoulders, I wave him on. "Come on, Jameson. We've got an archway to assemble."

I can play nice with Will. For Ava's sake, of course.

He crosses his arms and rocks back on his heels. "Did you just last-name me? Only my baseball coach does that."

I reach into the box and pull out two pieces of the golden contraption. "Sure did. And what does Will stand for? Wilbur?" I raise a brow. "Wilma?"

He smirks, letting his arms fall. "It's William, if you must know. And what about Morgan? What's that from? Maybe…the morgue?"

I make a face. "You need to work on your jokes."

He laughs, kneeling on the box's other side. "Yeah, not my best work."

"And, no." I pick up another bit of archway. "But that's where you'll end up if you don't help me with this."

His head snaps up, and he releases a low whistle. "Speaking of bad jokes…and death threats."

I laugh this time. "You're right. Enough with the subpar humor. Let's get to work." I place the two pieces on the floor. "Maybe we lay everything out and see if we can tell where they fit together?"

"Sounds good."

We spend the next forty-five minutes unloading the box, spreading the golden metal pieces in an arc shape, and then fitting them together.

As we work, we talk about our families—he has two sisters who will arrive with his parents for the wedding tomorrow, and I'm an only child. Our favorite sports—his is baseball, and mine is volleyball. Our future plans—he's headed to OU to study engineering, and I have no idea. Our church youth groups—mine, big, his, small. And more. I've almost forgotten Leo's unanswered text in my pocket. Almost.

I try not to, but I find myself watching Will when he's not looking. I'm distracted and entertained by the determined tilt to his brow and the satisfied smile that crosses his lips each time he finds a place for one of the shining pieces. He almost cheers when we stand the archway upright and, with the intricate golden vines woven together, it doesn't fall over.

He's cute when he's focused. Yikes! Where'd *that* unwanted thought come from?

He catches my grin, then frowns at the metal piece in his hand. "What?"

"You're enjoying this."

"Maybe." He holds up a hand and pinches two fingers together. "A little."

When he affixes the piece onto the archway and lets out an exaggerated whoop, I can't help but chuckle. "Only a little?"

"It's like we're playing an intense game of high-stakes wedding Tetris. No instructions. No rules. No option to fail." He lifts both palms. "What's not to love?"

I shake my head. "Whatever you say."

The golden archway comes together, but just when I think we're done, I find an odd piece still nestled in the box. I pick it up and rotate it in my hands.

"Uh, Will?" I say, holding up the mysterious piece. "Any ideas?"

He squints at it. "No. What'd we do wrong?" He takes it from me and walks around the archway. "Maybe here? No, that's not it."

We spend several intense minutes trying to figure out where it's intended to fit. The crease between his brow deepens.

I bite my lips to keep from smiling at his obvious frustration.

"What?" he says again.

"This is driving you crazy."

"No, it's not."

"Uh-huh." I eye the piece still clutched in his hand. "Well, what do we do?"

"Take the whole thing apart and try again?"

I cross my arms, bunching up my bridesmaid shirt. "Not a chance."

"Yeah. That would be crazy. And clearly, I'm not that."

"Clearly." I stoop to investigate the box one more time.

"Should we...hide it?"

I stand, smooth down my untucked shirt, and sweep my hair over my back. "But what if it collapses during the ceremony?"

He grips the arch, giving it a good shake. "Seems okay to me. Nobody will know." A mischievous glint brightens his dark eyes when he knows my protests have crumbled. He nods toward a discreet side door. "Stick it in the closet?"

I shake the arch too. "I suppose."

Will opens the door, and we step inside the tight space. He tosses the spare piece on one of the back shelves and pulls a box of communion packets in front of it. "Perfect."

"You're way too happy about this level of corruption."

He laughs, and we're both grinning when we return to the sanctuary.

"There you are." A voice cuts through the silence. A cute girl I vaguely recognize points between Will and me. She narrows her eyes, adjusts the camera strap slung over her pink cousin-of-the-groom T-shirt, and grins. "And what were you two doing in there?"

"Nothing," we both say at the same time.

She raises a brow.

"Hiding a leftover piece of the archway?" Will lifts his palms.

I gasp. "Will. Secret!"

He lowers his hands and tugs me closer. "Making out?"

My mouth drops open. You've got to be kidding me.

The girl laughs, and my cheeks flame.

"Definitely not," I say through clenched teeth, pushing him away.

"Relax, Morgan. I'm kidding." He chuckles. "This is my cousin, Emma. Our secrets are safe with her."

Emma nods to the closet door. "So you really did hide a piece of that archway in there?"

"Maybe. Maybe not. We'll never tell."

"You literally just did," Emma says.

He just shrugs.

She shakes her head and sticks her hand out in my direction. "Hey, I'm Emma."

"Morgan." I give her hand a shake. "You're the romance author."

"Yeah." Emma brightens. "Among other things."

"I told her she should read your book."

"Ah, thanks. So you're a reader?" She scoots closer, her camera swinging.

"Yep. And, actually, I already bought it. I'll start it tonight."

His head jerks back. "When did you do that?"

"Right after you told me about it. I bought it on my phone while we were ignoring each other on our way here."

"Ah. Right. Good times."

"Thanks so much for buying it." She claps, bouncing on her toes. "Even if it was at the recommendation of someone who spilled an ICEE all over you."

His eyes go wide. "Seriously. Does everyone know about that?"

"Of course."

"And I didn't spill it on her. We ran into each other. Whatever. What are you doing here anyway? Aren't you supposed to be on a boat somewhere?"

"I decided to hang back and take some photos." She holds up her sleek black camera. "I haven't been here in the summertime for years. I forgot how pretty it is. Morgan, how do you like Carlton Landing?"

"Love it. It's not what I expected."

"It's the perfect place to get away and relax. I always used to say the only thing it lacks is some sort of library or bookstore."

"I can see how it would be relaxing in a different situation. Weddings are a lot of work."

"Well, what are you guys up to? Besides making out in the closet or hiding something, allegedly."

Will huffs. "We volunteered to help today, so Ava and Hudson don't have to worry about it."

"That was nice. Maybe I'll help after I get more shots. I'm gathering photos for my Instagram portfolio. See you guys in a while?"

"Sure," Will says.

She leaves, and he whooshes out a breath, shoulders drooping.

"You know, you don't have to help. I can take care of stuff if you want to go do something fun."

He rubs the back of his neck. "No, I'm good. But we both should fit in something fun. Maybe as a reward for finishing the next job."

"I don't know. There's so much to do."

"Let's knock out the rest of the wedding favors, then take a short break."

"Short?"

"Yes, short."

"Okay. What would we do?"

He puts his palms together and gives me a pleading look. "Stand-up paddleboard?"

"I already told you I don't know how."

"That's the point. I'll teach you."

"That doesn't sound quick."

"It can be. Especially if we don't fall in."

I rock back on my heels. So far, this has been more of a fall-down kind of day. "I don't know."

"Okay, how about this, then? We divide the favors evenly. If I finish mine first, we paddleboard. If you finish yours first, you pick the activity."

"Interesting." I'm better than he is at assembling the favors. "But if I fall in, I'll have to change and deal with my wet hair."

"You think I won't?" He points at his dark-brown curls.

"You know what you're doing. You won't fall in."

"Okay, fine. If I win, we paddleboard, and you don't have to stand up if you don't want to. You can sit on the board."

"Okay, fine," I mimic. "But it doesn't matter because I'm going to win. And the wedding favors have to look good. We can't just throw them together."

He puts out a hand. "It's on."

We shake, he retrieves the two boxes from the golf cart, and we sit down to begin.

"Don't you want to know which activity I'll pick if I win?"

"Nope. Moot point. I'm going to win."

Sadly, he's right.

13

The paddleboard wobbles as I try to step onto it from the shallows near the beach. Below me, Lake Eufaula's reddish water looks ready to swallow me up. I double-check the buckles on my life jacket.

"Just have a seat like you're on a kayak." Will hands me the two-sided paddle, and I flop down with all the grace of my uncle James, trying to climb up on his tanning mat in the pool.

Once I'm settled, Will shoves the board, and I float out onto the water. I'm expecting immediate capsize, but I feel steady. Very steady. How does a blow-up board feel this sturdy? I run my hand over the surface. It's rigid and unyielding, not at all like a pool float.

Will must see my surprise because he says, "Told you it wasn't that hard."

He's right—*again*—though I'm not about to tell him so. It's almost like I'm sitting on the ground. Since the beach is nestled on a narrow stretch of lake—a jagged finger of the larger body of water—it's well protected from the Oklahoma wind, and the water is still.

"Come on. Let's go this way." Will is already standing, paddle in hand, perfectly balanced. He makes it look as easy as walking down the street. Meanwhile, I'm sitting crisscross applesauce like a first grader.

As he glides away, I dip my paddle in, pulling myself along on one side and then the other back and forth until I'm keeping pace.

A smile crosses my lips as the breeze ruffles my hair. This is actually…fun.

I follow him along the shore beyond the beach. Turtles dive off rocks and fallen logs, tiny fish swim below the surface, and birds chirp from the trees. This is a whole new way of exploring the world. A laugh burst loose, and I whisper, "I love this."

We point out bits of hidden nature as we float along until Will leads me away from the shore. He turns his board to face me, a challenge hardening his jaw. "You ready to stand up?"

"Um. I don't know." Am I? I mean, it doesn't seem hard.

"You can always sit back down if you don't like it."
He sits like me and then maneuvers onto his knees.
"Start like this."

"It's hard to take you seriously when you're wearing
swim trunks covered with multicolored catfish."

He smirks. "My options were limited. Stop stalling."

"Okay." Deep breath. I steady myself and move onto
my knees.

"Now tighten your core and center your body over
the board."

The hot Oklahoma sun beats down as I will my legs
to stay steady. I can do this.

"Just stand up nice and slow. Keep your eyes focused
on the shore."

I fix my gaze on the far shore, a mix of scrubby trees
and red dirt rocks. And slowly, shakily, I rise to my feet.
The board wobbles, but I bend my knees and find my
balance.

"There you go!" He grins. "Not so bad, right?"

I bite my lip, still not quite believing I'm standing on
this thing. "No, not bad."

He paddles closer, his muscular arms propelling him
through the water with ease. That thin braided bracelet
slides down his wrist. I tear my gaze away from his
tanned biceps before he notices my staring.

"Okay, now try paddling. Nice and slow."

I skim my paddle along the surface, intent on staying
upright. Like one of my grandpa's newborn baby
calves, all wobbly knees and elbows, I must look

ridiculous. I eye Will, self-conscious, but he's watching me with excitement and maybe pride. He nods, so I keep going, paddling once on one side of my board and then the other.

I begin to relax my tense shoulders, and once again, I'm smiling.

"See! I knew you could do it. Fun, right?"

My paddle and my own strength propel me across the top of the lake. "I hate it when you're right."

He snorts. "I'll try not to gloat. Too much."

We continue along in the deeper parts of this section until we reach the edge of the no-wake zone.

I pause and roll out my shoulders. "We better get back to work."

Will lets out an exaggerated huff. "I hate it when you're right."

I start to say something snarky, but my lips part when a bright-blue speedboat closes in. It's not heading at us, but a boat going that fast will send a wake.

"What is it?" Will turns back around. "Oh." He grips his paddle. "Bend your knees and ride it out."

The boat speeds to the wake zone and banks. When its engine quiets, its nose dips toward the water as it slows. Waves surge out behind it and roll in our direction.

I scramble into a seated position.

"You've got this. Bend your knees." Will looks over his shoulder. As he nods his approval at my new posture, the wave swells under his board. His foot slips, and he splashes into the water.

I grip the edge of my board as it surges upward and then down again.

Will's life jacket propels him upward, and his stunned face bobs above the surface.

"Sorry!" the boat driver yells as he rumbles past.

Will gapes in his direction, and I can't help but laugh. The waves become ripples, and I loosen my grip and lie back on the board, giggling.

"Think that's funny, huh?" Smiling, he swims in my direction. His board, attached to his ankle, follows along. "Will you laugh so hard if I tump you over?"

He grabs the edge of my board, and I sit up, trying to put on a serious face. "No, please. I beg you. My hair! It took an hour to straighten it this morning, and rehearsal dinner is tonight."

He pauses, hands ready to send me over.

I grip the edge. "Please. And we've already been out here too long. I'll lose another hour."

He loosens his grip. I let out a long breath. My mouth slides into a grin, but I don't dare voice my win lest he change his mind.

His wet face shines up at me, and his smile indicates he knows what I'm thinking. Point, Morgan. "Don't look so shocked. When I'm not sleep-and-luggage deprived, I'm a pretty nice guy."

I snort a derisive laugh but find I can't force my gaze away.

Water droplets have gathered on his lashes, and he brushes at the hair plastered to his forehead. The water makes it appear almost black. I reach out to help him push it away from his eyes. We lock gazes, and his expression changes.

I snatch my hand back. What am I doing? I shouldn't be touching his hair. Wasn't I supposed to loathe him when no one is around? That's the deal I made with him last night.

He pulls his paddleboard closer and reclaims his carefree smile. "Just know only your beautiful brown locks saved you today. Otherwise"—he points down at the water—"red-dirt bath."

"Noted."

He pushes away from me and flops onto his board.

I stay seated as we paddle toward the shore. Just what was that thrill as the word *beautiful* left his lips?

14

Will

The ham-and-cheese sandwich I bought at a converted Airstream food truck dumps a pile of shredded lettuce onto the concrete floor as I reach up one-handed to string twinkle lights through the wooden beams overhead. This isn't working.

I secure the lights and then stuff the rest of the sandwich into my mouth.

Also balanced on a chair in the lakeside pavilion, Morgan strings the other end of the lights. She reaches up on her tiptoes as a breeze blows wisps of hair across her shoulders. The lake sparkles behind her. Man, she's beautiful. Did she notice the electricity thrumming between us on the lake?

She must've because she's been distant ever since.

Before she catches me staring, I crane to survey our handiwork.

Not bad.

This open-air space will host the rehearsal dinner tonight as well as the reception and dance after the wedding tomorrow. Our instructions say to put only a few lights up now and then add the rest, plus an assortment of other decorations, tomorrow.

That list's all we have to go on, and we're doing our best. I hope it's good enough.

Morgan steps from her chair and pulls her phone from her back pocket. Her shoulders droop. "You've got to be kidding me."

"What is it?" I jump down and push the lettuce off the pavilion with my foot.

"Listen to this from Fran." She reads from the screen. "'The groom's ring needs to be picked up from the jeweler before two. That's when they close.'"

I check my phone. "It's already one fifteen. Yikes."

Morgan fishes the checklist from her pocket. She scans the front and then flips it over. "Yep. It's here. Lakeside Jewelry Store. But it doesn't say anything about two. I hadn't even read down this far. Do you think it's nearby?"

"I doubt it." I'm already searching in my map application. "It's twenty-five minutes away. We should go."

She turns the paper sideways. "There's an extra note. 'Owners require in-person pickup by bride and groom.'

Well, that's unfortunate. I'll text Fran." Her thumbs fly over her phone, and a moment later, she reads, "'We're too far out to come back in time. You'll have to fake it. They've never seen Morgan or Will, so it should be easy. Hudson says you can take his truck to save your gas money.'"

I quirk an eyebrow. "Is she saying what I think she's saying? We're going to pretend to be the bride and groom?"

"That's *exactly* what she's saying."

"Well." I cross my arms. "Think you can pretend to like me for, say, ten minutes?"

She rolls her eyes. "Doubt it. But we'll give it a go." She nods toward the strings of lights at her feet. "Should we leave this here?"

"Yeah. It'll be fine. We'll be right back. I can drive, but I need to grab my wallet."

She tugs at her shirt, wiggling the gold word *bridesmaid*. "We'll need to change too. Better break the Fish Eufaula shirt back out."

I groan. Will my parents ever get here with my suitcase?

Ten minutes later, we're changed and jogging to the public parking lot where Hudson's truck roasts in the sun. Morgan's staring at her car and the barely visible blue streaks still marring the driver's side door. She's quiet as I slide in behind the wheel and roll down the windows. So much has changed in a day. Is she remembering when I yelled at her, called her a psycho, or ruined her shoes? Not wanting to bring it up, I opt for silence as I guide us out of Carlton Landing.

When we hit Highway 9, we're both singing along to a 2000s-era country song about small-town life. I'd put it on expecting her to complain, but to my surprise, she started singing. She's propped her arm on the door, letting the wind race through her fingers.

Mine drum along on my steering wheel. "When I was younger, my parents played this song every time we drove into Carlton Landing. It sort of became our vacation-theme song. I still play it even if I'm by myself."

She smiles at this. "This is a great song for that."

When it ends and another one by the same band starts up, I turn it down. "So, what's our engagement story? I mean, that's usually the thing people ask, right?"

"Right. Good question. We could go with Ava and Hudson's engagement story."

"Do you know how it happened? I think they were at Carlton Landing, but that's all I know."

"Oh, it was great." Her eyes light up. "Ava said Hudson brought her out here to something called Porch Fest for a weekend. It was during my spring break. They stayed with your grandparents', and they helped him pull it off. The two of them went out on a boat where he asked her. And when they came back in, a romantic dinner was waiting under the stars. Lots of twinkle lights. One of the Porch Fest bands played for them. That's partly why they wanted to get married here."

"Good story. And now it's our story."

"No, it's *their* story. The two people we're pretending to be." She fiddles with the hem of her new Carlton Landing T-shirt she bought during our lunch break. "Our story is quite different."

I frown. Yeah, our story is interesting. It started badly, and it keeps getting more and more complicated. We're about to pretend to be engaged. It doesn't get much more complicated. But…somehow, it hasn't been as bad as I thought. At least not when she forgets she's supposed to hate me. Those are the confusing times. The times I forget *I'm* not open to this setup or a long-distance relationship. I'd do well to remember.

My phone blurts the next set of instructions, and I guide us into downtown Eufaula. I would consider this a small Oklahoma town, but it's much bigger than Carlton Landing. And much more established, whereas Mema told me Carlton Landing started in 2013. As far as rural Oklahoma goes, it's an infant.

"Arrived," my phone speaks as we pull into one of the two parking spots dedicated to Lakeside Jewelers.

We sit, neither of us wanting to move.

She shifts in her seat. "Don't we look a bit young to be getting married? What if they ask?"

"We can pass for upper college. We'll say we both just graduated."

"I guess." She lets out a slow breath. She's got freckles across her nose. Cute. "This is so bizarre. Sorry, you got stuck with this. With me."

I grip the steering wheel and smile. "It's not so bad. I volunteered, remember? And don't forget, the happy couple owes us. Big time." I kill the engine and pocket the keys. "Well, ready—cupcake?"

Her gaze flashes my way. She raises a brow.

"No? Pumpkin?"

"No," she says, deadpan.

"I'll think of something awesome."

She shakes her head and pushes her door open. Yep, she's trying to hide a smile.

We meet at the front of the truck, and I can't hide my surprise when she threads her fingers through mine.

A giggle tumbles from her lips. "Starting now, you'll have to be a better actor."

Her hand squeezes mine, and I don't hate it. "Right."

This day just gets more absurd by the minute.

15

Morgan

A bell jingles merrily as we enter the little shop, and I'm hyperaware of Will's palm pressed against mine.

An older man pops up from behind the counter, his eyes lighting up. "You must be the happy couple!" At our surprised faces, he continues. "My wife called someone named"—he lifts a paper from the counter and slides his glasses onto his nose—"Fran a few minutes ago to make sure you remember we close at two. She said you were on your way. So glad you made it!"

"Me too," I say. "Sorry to show up last minute. If the ring is ready, we'll get going so you can close up."

"Oh, nonsense." A plump woman bustles into the room, gripping a camera. "We have plenty of time for all our happy couples."

She places her hand on her chest. "Oh my, you two are young, aren't you?" But before we can respond, she perches herself on a stool next to a display case where she props her elbow. "So, how did you get engaged?"

Prepared for this one, Will tells the story brilliantly. The woman sits in rapt attention, crooning in all the right places. Her husband hovers nearby, listening.

The woman rests her chin in her hand. "And how did you meet? Have you known each other long?"

Okay. We weren't prepared for *that* one.

"Um," I say, ever the eloquent one. And my palm starts to sweat in this interrogation room. One wrong move, they'll toss us out of Oklahoma. I'm *so* not good at this.

"Well," he drawls, "it was a bad beginning. We were both in a hurry—to go to the same place, as it turns out—and bumped into each other. We spilled our drinks all over our clothes and shoes."

"Oh my! What a meet-cute."

"It wasn't very cute, to be honest, and when we arrived at the place we were going and saw the other there, neither of us was very happy. But fast forward a bit, and here we are."

The woman puts her hand over her chest again. "Oh, a romance born of tragedy." She bats her eyes at her husband. "It reminds me of your story."

He comes to stand behind her, gnarled hands gripping her shoulders. "We had a similar mishap the first time we met. But it was a small price to pay for the last forty-five years."

He squeezes her shoulders, and leaning her head back into him, she giggles in a girlish manner. Then she frowns at our linked hands.

"Where's your ring, dear?" she asks me.

I hadn't thought of that either. "Well…" I swallow. "We went paddleboarding, and I didn't want to risk losing it. I didn't have time to grab it before we rushed here."

Will meets my eyes and nods in approval.

"Oh, too bad. I love engagement rings. Do think of us if you ever have any other jewelry needs."

"Sure." Will's lips twitch with a suppressed smile.

"Speaking of jewelry." The man holds up a small box. "I have your freshly cleaned and polished groom's ring right here."

Will reaches for it, but the man pulls it back. "We have a special tradition here. Before we hand over the goods, we need a photo of the bride and groom for our wedding collage." He gestures to a collage of photos covering the back wall.

I should've known.

No problem. We can do this. I grip Will's hand as the woman directs us into the light.

"That's right, stand right there."

Will smooths out his bright-yellow Fish Eufaula T-shirt and floppy curls. "I'm not dressed for this."

The man chuckles. "You're looking sharp, son. I have that same shirt."

Will catches my eye, and I try not to laugh.

The woman adjusts my hair and then steps back. "Now, give us a nice big smile."

We lean toward each other, and she snaps a few Polaroids. That wasn't so bad. We start to move away when she says, "All right, let's see some love now. Give us a kiss for the camera."

Will and I exchange wide-eyed glances, our hands still linked together. My heart begins to race as I try to stifle my panic. *This* was not part of the plan. And if I'm not mistaken, Will is every bit as shocked as I am.

"Um." He hesitates, his deep brown eyes searching mine. "We're pretty private. I don't think—"

"Bah." The man waves at this. "Don't be silly."

"Besides," the woman sings merrily, utterly unaware of our discomfort, "no kiss, no ring, and it's closing time."

She positions her camera, and Will squeezes my hand ever so slightly. Is this his way of asking permission?

"Come on now. Don't be bashful." The woman winks. "It's tradition!"

I turn toward Will at the moment he shifts toward me. Our faces are inches apart. My breath hitches as his wide brown eyes seem to draw me in. He releases my hand and slides his fingers up my arm to my elbow. Of its own accord, my hand moves to brush his side. He lifts a brow, a question on his face.

"Okay," I whisper, my voice barely audible.

He leans toward me, and my eyes drift closed. Our lips meet hesitantly at first, the initial contact sending unexpected sparks through my body. As his lips move against mine, all thoughts of our current predicament fade. I rise onto my toes, my fingers gripping his hideous shirt. His free hand moves to my neck, his thumb brushing my jaw. And what was supposed to be a brief moment turns into something else.

When our lips finally separate and my eyelids flutter open, neither of us moves away.

Wow.

"All right. That's enough, lovebirds!" The man's laughter breaks through our reverie, causing us to jump apart. "I thought you were private." He chortles again, and my cheeks burn as I attempt to steady my breathing.

"Sorry," I mutter. Could today be more embarrassing?

The woman continues to snap photos. "Oh, we know what it's like to be young and in love."

Will chuckles, and I track the feeling as his hand slides back down my forearm to intertwine our fingers again.

"Here you go." The man hands over the ring and a few photos. "We wish you all the best."

Will takes them, and the woman ushers us toward the door. "Yes, have a lovely wedding day. And do drive carefully."

"Thank you. We will." Will's voice is steadier than I expect, seeing as I still don't trust myself to put coherent words together.

He pockets the ring and opens the door with a ding, pulling me out onto the sidewalk. After one more wave, the woman locks up.

We stand, linked by our fingers, staring at Hudson's familiar truck.

"Well—" Will starts, but he can't seem to find the right words.

"Yeah." Apparently, neither can I.

He releases my hand, and we separate, walking to each side of the cab. Our gazes meet briefly over the hood. As we slide into our seats, I press my fingers to my still-tingling lips.

That was…unexpected.

16

Will

The sun blazes in the afternoon sky, casting sharp blades of light over the crooked road as we drive back into Carlton Landing. A palpable tension overrides our silence, both of us reeling. Or at least I am.

I grip the steering wheel, knuckles white. I should say something. Anything. But what?

She seems lost in thought. With the open and vulnerable expression from earlier gone, her indifferent mask is back in place.

The breeze rustles her hair as she faces the open passenger window. Her tropical scent drifts my way while her fingers tap a nervous beat to the song issuing from Hudson's crappy speakers.

I turn up the volume, the only thing that seems capable of cutting through the thick nothing between us, and try not to let my mind wander back to the jewelry shop. But I can't seem to help it. The moment she squeezed my fingers. When she turned my way, gaze dipping to my lips. Her resigned expression. Her soft lips teasing mine.

And then another expression when we pulled apart. Surprise?

And was it a good surprise or a bad surprise?

I breathe in the coconut and flowers. I should put the whole thing out of my mind. It was all an act. Right?

Okay, I can admit it. I'm starting to like her, but we're going in opposite directions after this wedding. What am I doing, letting these thoughts run through my head?

So, when my mind starts to replay the scene yet again, I paddle it out of dangerous waters. We're nearing the crest of the hill. "Did you get to go out on the lookout when you came into town?"

"No." Morgan leans forward in her seat, twisting a lock of dark hair around her finger. "I haven't been out there yet."

"Want to?"

She wobbles a smile onto those pliable heart-shaped lips. "Yeah. Let's do it."

I veer onto a gravel parking area and cut the engine. Morgan steps out and wanders past the four white Adirondack chairs and toward the edge. I follow, hands shoved in my pockets. The awkwardness hasn't died. But maybe it's easing.

The lake shimmers below, surrounded edge to edge by trees. A few houses peek above the forest farther down the shoreline, white, yellow, gray, and even shocking blue.

Morgan fills her lungs and then slowly lets it out. "Wow, it's beautiful up here."

"I've always loved it." I grin, and she smiles back.

We step onto one of the boulders lining the grassy area and take in the Oklahoma landscape.

The sun highlights her profile, sending pink cheeks aglow. What's she thinking?

She hops onto the next rock, and it teeters, rocking forward under her weight. She stumbles, her arms flailing with her attempt to regain her balance. My reflexes kick in, and I catch her hand and yank her back to me, wrapping my other arm around her waist. She crashes into my chest where her hand splays. We're back on sturdy ground, and she's blinking up at me, her brown eyes wide. Freckles play peekaboo behind the strands of hair caressing her face.

"You okay?" My breath moves the hair from her forehead. Hers warms my neck, the sensation oh-so-sweet.

"Y–yeah," she stammers. "Thanks."

She jitters back a bit and pushes the hair from her face. We stare at each other, and something shifts in the atmosphere. It feels like the exact opposite of putting her out of my mind.

Before either of us finds anything to say, a ridiculously upbeat love song blares from her pocket and grounds the sudden electricity. I step back as she wiggles her phone free. The word *Leo* flashes on her screen before she silences the sound and shoves it back into her pocket.

Then gravel crunches nearby.

"Will? Morgan?" Ava calls out from a golf cart, and Hudson parks next to my—well, *his*—truck. "What are you doing up here?"

I jam my hands back in my pockets and toe a pebble off the boulder. It clatters down, down, down the cliff. "Morgan hadn't been out here yet, so we decided to take a look on our way back into town."

They join us, and Hudson crosses his arms, bunching his green groom shirt. "My favorite spot in Carlton Landing." He elbows Morgan. "So what do you think?"

Shading her eyes, one hand pinning down her glossy hair, she exhales a deep satisfied sound. "Same. New favorite spot. I'm surprised you're not getting married up here."

"We did think about that." Ava saunters closer. "I think people do pretty often. But in the end, we wanted a church wedding. Plus, the Oklahoma wind is hard to predict."

Hudson steps onto Morgan's unsteady rock, and we both yell, "No!"

"What?" He pretends to ride a surfboard, rocking it back and forth with his body weight.

"Hudson! What are you doing? No broken legs the day before our wedding." Ava holds out a hand, and he grabs it, jumps down, snugs her close, and plants a kiss on her forehead.

Morgan lets out a breath.

I shake my head. "Morgan nearly killed herself on that thing. She almost fell down the hill."

Hudson releases Ava. "Nah, a tree would've stopped her fall."

"Thanks, Hudson." Morgan tucks wayward hair behind her ears. "That's comforting."

Ava pats him on the back, heads over to the chairs, and plops into one. We follow and do the same, leaning our heads back and relaxing in the sun.

Morgan tells them about the jewelers. Her gaze flicks to mine before she omits the part where we kiss. Our little secret, then.

Crossing her ankles, Ava stretches out. "I can't believe they took your photo! Did you get to keep one?"

"No, I didn't keep any," Morgan says.

That's true. *She* didn't keep them. She shoved them in the glove box and probably intends to toss them when we get back to town.

"Did you pull it off, or did you break character?" Hudson bounces his knee.

"I think we sold it pretty well." I rub my jaw. "The lady asked a lot of questions, though. Like how I proposed."

"What did you say?"

"I told them your story."

"Nice." Hudson gives me a fist bump. "And thanks for doing that. I forgot they close at two."

"No problem." Lacing her fingers behind her head, Morgan closes her eyes against the bright sun. "So, how was the boating trip?"

Ava taps on the smooth wood armrests. "It was fun but crowded. We just got back and wanted some space."

"Never thought we'd run into you two up here." Hudson waggles his eyebrows.

"Hudson, stop bugging them." Groaning, Ava slaps his arm. "Leave them alone."

"Fine." He reaches over to clap me on the shoulder. "Ready to head down for the bocce ball tournament?"

That sounds fun. Morgan squints open one eye. Her head rocking my way, she nods as if giving me permission, but her tired face prompts me to say, "Thanks, but I'll help Morgan with the lights on the pavilion."

Her eyes go wide, and after a beat, I tense. Oops.

Ava frowns. "What do you mean?"

Morgan cringes, and her shoulders inch up by her ears. "It's—part of the surprise?"

"Ava, were you helping Evelyn decorate for the reception? You don't need to do that. We're paying her to take care of everything."

Mouth hanging open, Morgan can't seem to find her voice. Finally, she squirms. "It's fine. Evelyn didn't—"

She doesn't have to finish the lie because Ava's phone rings, and she holds up a finger. "Hold that thought." She slides that finger across the screen. "Hey, Mom."

"Okay, honey." Over speakerphone, Fran's irritating voice is even more grating. "Cat's out of the bag. Uncle Byron found out and told everybody."

"Told everybody what?"

"That Evelyn left."

"She *left?*" Ava jolts upright, her voice rising an octave. "When?"

"Now, don't freak out like your dad. Everything will be just fine. Morgan and that boy have been working on things all day."

My brows push up into my hair. That boy?

Ava stands and begins to pace in front of the chairs. "All day?"

"Evelyn left last night. She didn't feel well."

"Last night?" Ava rakes through her spa-fresh hair. "Why didn't you tell me?"

"Because of this right here. I didn't want any drama." Someone starts talking to Fran in the background. "I have to go, honey. We'll talk more in a bit."

The call ends.

There's silence except for the wind and birdcalls. Ava's frozen, clutching her phone. "Is she serious? Have you been working all day?"

Morgan nods. "But it's okay. I wanted to help."

Ava shoves her phone into her back pocket. "Wait. Is this why you didn't go on the boat?"

"Maaay–be?"

Ava palms her cheeks. "I'm so sorry. I can't believe this. I can't believe she put you to work without even telling me." She spins to me. "And you too!"

Morgan stands. "Your mom asked me to do it. Will volunteered to help me."

Hudson gives me a knowing smirk. "Nice."

"Not the time, Hudson," Ava snaps, pacing again.

"And Evelyn didn't abandon you." Standing, I brush debris off my blue-stained shorts. "She left in an ambulance last night."

We fill her in. Then she insists on hearing how we became Fran's minions.

When we finish, she grips each of our shoulders. "I'm so sorry. But don't worry. Hudson and I are going to help now. You won't have to be stuck together anymore."

That doesn't sit as well as it should. Sure, it'll be nice to have help with the never-ending list. Still, it grates to think of someone actively preventing me from being *stuck* with Morgan.

As I try to gauge her reaction, she just smiles and nods. Is she… relieved? That doesn't sit well, either.

"Thanks, Ava," she says. "And I didn't mind. I want your big day to be perfect."

Ava seems near tears now, so Hudson rubs his hands together. "Okay, I'll tell Matt the bocce ball tournament is off. What do we need to do first?"

"Sounds like the pavilion needs work. Maybe we finish that first?" Ava says.

He nods. "All right. Let's get going."

Ava grabs Morgan's hand and tugs her away. "You can ride with me in the golf cart."

They trot off.

Hudson twitches his fingers for the keys. "Guess you're with me."

I hand them over as Morgan and Ava drive away. Great. He's watching me with a stupid I-see-what's-happening-here smirk.

"What?"

"Oh, nothing. I am just thinking about how you and Morgan seem different since this morning. Something going on you want to share with your dear cousin?"

I rake a hand through my hair. "Don't start. Nothing's going on."

But he grins, clapping me on the back. "Sure, there's not. All I'm saying is maybe it's time to stop pining for that other girl who keeps stringing you along—what's her name? Scarlet? Instead, look at what's right in front of you. And I'll remind you *again* that Morgan doesn't live that far from OU."

I shake my head as we slide into the truck cab. "She seemed pretty happy to get away from me. Plus, I don't do setups, remember?"

But I hadn't thought of Scarlet all day.

He shrugs, still smirking. Know-it-all. "Does Morgan seem like the other girls you've been set up with?"

I don't answer as their cart disappears down the road. No, Morgan's not like them at all. But she still hates me —and gets phone calls from some guy named Leo.

With a huff, I roll up the window. "What do you know about Leo?"

Did I honestly ask that?

Hudson's smug laugh makes me want to toss him in the lake. "Now, why would my *uninterested* cousin want to know about him?"

17

Morgan

The wind whips through my hair as Ava and I cruise along the sloping road toward town. Snippets of the sparkling lake flash through the trees. As the quaint houses come into view, the sun reflects off their metal rooftops, creating a dazzling, postcard-worthy scene that should leave me mesmerized. But instead of enjoying *this* moment, I'm enjoying another—our unexpected kiss at the jewelry shop.

What did he make of it? Does he regret it? Is he telling Hudson about it now and laughing about the awkwardness?

I fiddle with the frayed edge of my jean shorts. Maybe I need to talk it out. Should I tell Ava?

Her hair dances in the breeze, creating a wild blonde frame for the worry lines creasing her brow. I can't bring myself to introduce more unnecessary drama to her wedding weekend. Not to mention, this is the definition of stealing someone's thunder. I don't want her focused on me and my problems. So I keep my secret locked away, hidden behind a forced smile.

But Ava has other ideas.

As we bump across the stone bridge, she nudges me. "You seem a bit off this afternoon. What's going on?"

Smile, right? I paste it back in place. I'll tell her everything later—like in a few years. "Nothing. I'm just tired."

"Are you mad at me for not saving you from my mom earlier?"

Whoa! I hold up both hands. "No, not at all. How could I possibly be mad at you? And like I said, I don't mind helping."

Her shoulders relax, and she checks her makeup in the rearview mirror. "And how was your afternoon with Will?"

"Fine."

She raises a perfectly manicured brow. The spa must've been nice. "Come on. Spill. Something's up with you two."

I pick at my shorts again. "Nothing's up."

"I don't know. I sensed some vibes earlier."

"Nope, no vibes." My laugh comes in a nervous jitter, and my heart somersaults over his lips on mine.

Get it together, Morgan! This weekend is complicated enough. Stop thinking about that kiss.

"We met yesterday. He's barely more than a stranger. I'm here for your wedding. That's all. It's going to be amazing, by the way. Wait until you see what we've done to the pavilion already." My subject change works, and we discuss the wedding and what still needs to be done.

As we stop in front of the pavilion, I twinge over not being honest.

How can I explain something I don't understand myself? I need to put it out of my mind. From now on, I'm focusing on the task—making her wedding perfect. And if that means keeping my emotions in check and forgetting the cute and confusing groomsman, then so be it.

And no thinking about the kiss. Again.

Ava pockets the keys. "All right, hand over the list."

I do, relieved to be rid of it.

"Now, let's get to work."

She spends a few minutes connecting her phone to the Bluetooth speaker in the pavilion until an upbeat country song drifts through the open space.

I pick up where I left off with the string of lights as the wind blows through my hair and rustles the leaves.

Elementary-age kids whiz by on their bikes.

"Looking good, ladies!" Hudson calls out, Will following, and my heart jumps into high gear.

Stop that. It was just a kiss. It was nothing.

Still, I expect him to help me like he's been doing all afternoon. Instead, he joins Hudson and stretches out a string of lights, and I get back at it. I grind my teeth. Why am I disappointed?

Everything is as it should be. We won't have to work together anymore, and I'm glad.

Good. Fine.

The rest of the wedding party catches wind of our predicament and shows up to help. Soon, we've stretched all the strands across the beams and pillars. We move on to setting up tables and assembling centerpieces. As we finish, Fran shows up to *help*.

"Oh, how lovely," she croons, walking around in her spiked heels, adjusting things as she sees fit. Once she's reworked three of the centerpieces, she declares the place ready and shoos us off to get dressed for rehearsal dinner. She doesn't even say thank you for our full day of work.

Forty-five minutes later, I've showered and arranged my hair into a messy but cute bun, applied some makeup, and stepped into the flowing lilac dress I brought just for this evening.

Tonya and two other newly arrived bridesmaids join Ava and me as we stroll along the boardwalk toward the chapel. Hudson and several groomsmen join us. Will isn't with them. I'm introduced to the newcomers, all college friends of Hudson and Ava. They know each other well, so I walk alone behind the chattering group.

The sun has dipped below the tree line, casting long shadows across our path, and the breeze teases loose curls around my face. The strung lights that hang year-round over the walkways between rows of houses glimmer.

I pull out my phone and open the messaging app. My parents said they'd check in this evening. Nothing yet.

"Morgan, wait up."

My breath catches as Will, showered and dressed to impress, jogs toward us. Toward *me*. His hair is still damp, making it look even darker. Charcoal pants and a crisp white button-up hug his frame, and he's shaved away the bit of stubble he had. I would know since his lips were on mine only hours ago.

Don't think about that.

I curl my toes against the urge to point my feet in the other direction and ignore him. How can I act normal around someone I unexpectedly locked lips with? This boy is wreaking havoc on my emotions.

But that would be rude.

I freeze on a smile and wait.

"Wow." He stops at my side. "You look beautiful."

I dip my head. I can't help it.

My cheeks must be pink, but desperate to act normal, I force my eyes back up. "Thank you. You look nice too. Where'd you get clothes?"

"My family arrived. Thank goodness." He trails the others, and I fall in step.

"Do you know the other bridesmaids?"

"Not really. Or at least I don't know them well. How about you? Do you know the other groomsmen?"

He twists his blue-and-white bracelet around his wrist. Something from an admirer? "Nope. I feel like the outsider."

"At least you know a lot of the family. I only know Fran."

He makes a face and lets his hands drop to his sides. "She's the worst."

"She really is."

He nods toward the group ahead. They haven't even looked back to see if we're here. "We're like their annoying and forgettable younger siblings."

"Maybe they'll set up a kids' table for us."

One corner of his mouth quirks up. "Maybe. When do your parents arrive?"

"Tomorrow, probably just before the ceremony." I stow my phone in my silver beaded clutch. "They're supposed to let me know their plan this evening."

We walk on in not-entirely-awkward silence until I spot our destination. "Oh, wow."

The deep-green forest hugs the chapel as the sun dips. In the shadows, its white exterior isn't quite as sharp. Soft golden light spills from gleaming windows.

"Yeah, and look at the pavilion." He points. Lights along the ground lead a path between the chapel and the glowing pavilion where our hours of labor are apparent.

"It looks amazing." I catch him staring at me.

He recovers, agreeing with my assessment. "Yeah. I heard their decorating crew is pretty good."

"Will. Morgan. Keep up," Fran calls from the doorway. "It's time."

We rush along, and she makes quick work of getting us to our starting positions. Emma takes candid photos of the rehearsal, including when we exit the sanctuary arm in arm after the first run-through.

"Ah, that's a good one," she says, looking at the screen on her camera.

Fran claps. "Not bad, but let's run through it again. Places, everyone."

Will groans, and I nudge him toward the other groomsmen.

We run through the ceremony two more times before Fran is satisfied. "That's a wrap, everyone." She beams. "Time to eat."

Hudson and Ava lead the way down the lit path toward the pavilion where the caterer has set up for our arrival. The crew bustles in and out of a nearby hut serving as the kitchen.

Once again, I find myself walking alone, this time sandwiched between different groups of family and friends.

My phone chirps inside my clutch, and I pull it free, expecting a text from my parents. Then conflicting emotions roil me. It's not from Mom.

Leo: I want to see you. Can we talk?

"Did your parents finally text?" Will sidles next to me.

I dim the screen and stow it away. Did he read it? "No, not yet."

We continue, walking side by side, and my only thought should be that I don't want to talk to Leo. And that's part of what I'm feeling—my emotions are a chaotic mess when it comes to him. But it's not my only thought.

I don't want to care, but if Will had time to read that text, what did he think?

I start to fish for something to say, but Leo's ringtone blares from my clutch. I slow to dig it out, but Will continues on.

I sigh. This confusion is a perfect reminder that I've sworn off dating until college.

I just need to keep my head on straight, get through this wedding, and stick to the plan. No dating. No weekend flings.

I send Leo's phone call to voicemail.

18

Will

I shuffle my feet and shove my hands in the pockets of my dress pants. Across the pavilion, Morgan's sitting alone at our table—not the kids' table, after all. Her purple dress flows to the floor, and the twinkle lights bathe her in a soft glow. Other guests chat and laugh, mingling to the gentle acoustic guitar chords, but Morgan traces the condensation on her lemonade glass, a deep crease between her brows. Man, even in her melancholy state, she's stunning.

She'd been quiet during dinner, and it probably has everything to do with that phone call. I didn't intend to see a text from her ex, but I did. And I recognized his stupid love-song ringtone.

Why hasn't she changed it by now?

"Will, do you think your parents should join the boat club?"

I return my attention to my uncle Charlie. "Sure. That would be fun."

He nods to Dad. "See? Your kids would love it. Worth every penny in the summertime."

I've been standing with Dad and Mema, listening to Uncle Charlie drone on—well, *half* listening. Most of my brainpower seems to be routed toward keeping my chin from swiveling in Morgan's direction. Not even the coveted boat club can claim my attention.

Everything feels different since that kiss, but while my heart and eyes linger on her lips, my head knows better. My brain has entered full-on self-preservation mode. Run the other way, it said. And so I did.

As soon as the meal ended, I left the table, mumbling some excuse about needing to talk to Mema. Emma sat between Morgan and me at dinner, and while we both chatted with Emma, Morgan and I barely said two words to each other the entire meal. Still, I have to keep reminding myself of all the reasons not to walk over there and see if she's okay.

One—she's a setup. Those never work.

Two—she lives far away and is in high school. I'm two months beyond that. Way too old for her.

Three—she doesn't even like me and is pining over that other guy. Leo or whatever.

I've never met the guy, but do know he broke her heart, so I'm not a fan.

Yeah. That's why I'm reacting this way. I'm protective of my new friend. And it's why I hate that he wants to reconnect.

Riiight.

I did what I had to do. I have feelings I don't want to have about a girl who is probably getting back with her ex. Self-preservation.

Morgan glances up, and I avert my gaze, pretending to be interested in Uncle Charlie's boat story. Is he *still* talking about that? Did she catch my staring?

Eventually, our group scatters, and I'm left standing alone on the edge of the festivities.

"You look lost over here." Hudson saunters over, his signature grin in place.

Emma follows, using her camera to boss everyone around. "Smile, you two."

I fake one, and she snaps a photo.

"What are you doing over here by yourself?" Hudson leans against a support beam.

"Just thinking," I mutter.

"About a certain bridesmaid, perhaps?" Emma frames another shot.

"What?" Why is everyone so nosy? I shove my rolled sleeves up my forearms. "No. Of course not."

He raises an eyebrow. "Uh-huh. Keep telling yourself that."

Emma snaps a photo of Morgan's stoic expression. "Why don't you go talk to her?"

"I don't want to."

"Yes, you do," Hudson says.

"What is this—an interrogation?"

Hudson grins. "Maybe. We're trying to get you to confess."

"Confess what?"

"That you're interested."

I roll my eyes. "I'm about to tell your fiancé on you. She told you to stop bugging me about this."

"Yes, but that was before I had evidence."

"What are you talking about now?"

"Emma. Show him exhibit A."

Emma flips her camera around and scrolls through her photos. She tilts it my way when she finds what she's looking for. This photo was taken earlier at rehearsal. Morgan and I are exiting the sanctuary arm in arm. Our heads are turned toward each other, and she's laughing. I'm gazing at her with an easy—some might say, infatuated—smile. Clearly, she has my full attention.

"So? I told a joke. She laughed. Big deal."

"Wait, there's more." She scrolls through photos in different settings—all of me gawking at or talking to Morgan. The last is from just a few minutes ago. Uncle Charlie is talking, and I'm staring across the room.

I laugh it off. "Emma, you're creepy. You know that, right? How did you even take that?"

"I'm creepy?" She swats at my arm. "*You're* the one staring at the beautiful girl who's sitting all alone. Maybe she's sad because you're ignoring her."

"She's been ignoring *me*."

Emma jams a fist onto her hip. "Go talk to her, big baby."

My eyes go wide at this. "Whoa. Rude."

She claps me on the shoulder. "Tough love, man. You need it."

I sigh and crane around again. This time, Morgan's looking at me, but she's quick to duck her head.

"Well, that was interesting," Hudson says. "As the cliché goes, you can cut the tension with a knife."

"Can't we please focus on your wedding? You're getting married tomorrow. Big day and all."

"I give you full permission to devote your attention to whatever's going on here." He indicates the vast space between Morgan and me.

"Admit it." Emma bumps me with her shoulder. "You like her."

"Okay, fine. I'm not not interested."

My—um, *well-meaning?*—cousins high-five in front of my face, and then Emma steps back to snap a too-close photo of me. "I knew it. Called it."

"You guys are so annoying."

"But you love us." He rubs his hands together. "So, what's the plan? What are you going to do?"

"Plan? There's no plan. She doesn't even like me. Plus, her ex-boyfriend keeps calling. Maybe she still likes him."

"Leo? That idiot? Nah." He nudges me in Morgan's direction. "Get over there, man."

I don't budge.

"All I'm saying is talk to her while you've got the chance. See where it goes. Maybe nowhere. Maybe somewhere. And a word of advice, give her a real apology for the ICEE incident, and especially the"—he pitches his voice low—"psycho comment."

Sitting alone, Morgan pleats the edge of the tablecloth. He's right, of course. My feeble whispered apology at dinner last night wasn't worth much. And I didn't even mean it. Before I have a chance to decide if I'll go over there, Fran swoops in and takes the seat next to Morgan, chattering away.

The three of us stare in their direction. Hudson groans.

I rock back on my heels. "Great. She's probably giving Morgan more to do."

"Looks like I'm going to have to take matters into my own hands." Hudson winks. Before I can ask what he means, he strides off.

"What's he going to do?" I ask Emma.

"No idea."

He approaches his fiancée and whispers in her ear. Ava nods, and a too-happy smile appears on her face.

"Oh no," I mutter.

They step onto the small stage at the front of the pavilion.

"Attention, everyone!" Ava announces.

I have the sudden urge to bolt. What's she about to say?

The guitar music halts, the crowd quiets, and Morgan and Fran turn in their seats.

I edge a step backward.

"We weren't planning to do this tonight, but Hudson and I have decided we should practice our first dance for the reception tomorrow."

I pause my retreat.

"If you can, we'd love for you to join in. Here's how it will go. We'll start it off, and after a minute or so, our parents and the bridal party should pair off and join us. Then, for the second song, everyone else should join in. Sound okay?"

With a buzz of agreement and excitement, people shuffle around the room.

Hudson leads Ava onto the dance floor and gives me a pointed glare when I'm slow to move from my spot. I try not to roll my eyes at his obvious matchmaking.

"Will," he calls out, "you'll be with Morgan."

Emma and I groan in unison. "Did no one teach you guys the art of subtlety?"

She giggles. "Well, he *is* Fran's future son-in-law. Now get over there before I call you a baby again."

I shake my head and approach Morgan. Fran is talking again.

"Hey." I try to sound casual, interrupting.

"Hi," Morgan replies, her deep-brown eyes reflecting my nervous image.

"Sorry, Mrs. Thompson. But I need to steal Morgan away."

"Oh, very well." She stands, craning her neck over the crowd. "I need to find my husband. We've been practicing!"

Relief floods Morgan's features as Fran retreats, heels click-clacking across the room.

I shuffle my feet. "Sounds like we're dance partners." *Really, Will?*

Morgan waves at Ava and Hudson, who gawk at us as they sway to the music. "I don't think we have a choice."

Based on that statement, I might think she didn't want to dance. But she's smiling, and laughter dances in her eyes.

I shrug. "Not when the creepy bride and groom are on a mission. Couple of stalkers." I don't voice what that mission is as I take her hand and lead her to the dance floor. She already knows.

19

Morgan

With my hand resting in Will's, we step out onto the dance floor alongside the rest of the wedding party. Will seems careful to avoid getting too close to Ava and Hudson, and by their smug looks, I can't blame him. I bet this was all an elaborate scheme to get us to dance together.

Point to the meddling couple.

Not letting go of my fingers, Will slides his other hand onto my lower back. His aftershave scent envelops me.

I run a hand over his shoulder, taking in the sharp angle of his jaw and the intensity in those deep-brown eyes. His curls graze my fingertips as my hand drifts toward his neck. I've been avoiding him this evening.

Not only because I still feel the awkwardness of our kiss hovering between us but also because I've been contemplating Leo's sudden attempts.

But Will's been avoiding me too.

My eyebrows draw together as I try to puzzle it out. Is he only standing here with me because Ava and Hudson forced it?

"What?" he says as we sway to the slow melody.

I further duck my head. "I'm trying to figure you out."

"Really? Any luck with that?"

I laugh. "No, definitely not."

"Good. I like being mysterious."

My fingers twitch, then tug at a hunk of his hair. "You're hopeless."

Will's younger sister darts past us, giggling. "Oooh, Will's dancing with a girl."

Will rolls his eyes, but his hand presses hard to my back. "You seemed pretty stoic all through dinner. Is everything okay?"

"Yeah, sorry. A lot on my mind."

"Ever since that phone call?"

Did he know who had called me? Surely not.

When I don't answer, he tries again. "Well, *is* everything okay?"

"I guess. It's just…" I let out a heavy breath, my shoulders drooping and my chest deflating. "You really want to know?"

His fingers tighten on mine, and his chin brushes my hair. "Yeah."

Not the moment to think of the kiss. To wonder what would happen if I tipped my head just so right now. I scoot further back and mumble, "It was my ex-boyfriend, Leo. I haven't heard from him in a while."

A muscle flexes in his jaw. "Oh? And what did Leon have to say?"

"Leo."

His mouth quirks up. "Whatever."

"You're as bad as Fran."

"Wow, that hurts."

I feign regret. "You're right. That was too far. I wouldn't sling that insult against my worst enemy."

He laughs and scoops me closer. "Good to know I'm not your *worst* enemy."

"No, not the worst."

We fall into silence until his next words burst out. "Well? What did Lenny have to say?"

I give him a look. "He's been texting and calling all weekend. He says he wants to see me."

Will pulls me in another direction to avoid bumping into Tonya and Matt, his back rigid. "And how do you feel about that?"

"I'm… not sure." I worry my lower lip through my teeth, avoiding his intense stare beneath those mesmerizing eyelashes. "It's complicated."

And that's the truth. So many emotions. Hurt is at the forefront. But sadness is there too. Embarrassment. And crazy enough, the memory of the love I used to feel. That's the worst because I don't want to feel it. To remember it.

Will doesn't reply right away, but I can sense his discontent with my answer. And why does he care anyway?

"How long did you date before you broke it off?"

"Well, *I* didn't break it off." The string of lights over his shoulder glints in my vision. His breath rustles the hair at my temple. Minty. "He did. At a wedding. A lot of people heard."

"Is that why you hate weddings?"

"That's part of it."

"There's more?"

Fran sashays by. She and her husband flow around the dance floor, putting everyone else to shame. She spins toward us. "As I was saying, Morgan. We could use your expertise this evening."

I try to respond, but Fran swirls away.

Will mutters, "Show off."

"Yep."

"So what was that about?"

"She wants me to bake cookies for brunch tomorrow. Not just any run-of-the-mill cookie. Full-on decorated sugar cookies like you buy from a bakery." Like people used to buy from me.

"But you don't want to. Because you don't bake anymore."

"Right."

"You ready to tell me why not?"

"Not really."

He tilts his head at the string lights and crossbeams. "Let's see. Maybe it's because—you suddenly developed a deadly sugar allergy."

"No, thank goodness. That sounds terrible."

"Or maybe you were abducted by aliens, and they made you bake for them—"

I release his fingers and press mine over his mouth. "Please don't finish that. I'll tell you."

He shrugs, one corner of his mouth quirking. His fingers flex against my back. "I'm good at wearing people down."

"And you think that's a good thing?"

"Stop stalling. Why don't you like to bake anymore? Didn't you work in a bakery?"

"Yes." We pause as a new song starts, beginning our dance again to a new rhythm. "I worked at a bakery specializing in wedding cakes. It was my dream job. At the time, I'd wanted to open my own bakery someday. We provided more than just wedding cakes, but those were the moneymakers, and that's why I wasn't allowed to help with them as a new employee. But my coworker got the flu, and I had to step in at the last minute."

"Oh wow. You *did* poison people, didn't you?"

"No. And I'm going to pretend you didn't say that. The short of it is we delivered the wedding cake and the groom's cake. As we were waiting around to bring them out at the right moment and start serving, Leo found me. Oh, did I mention this was the same wedding where I was dumped?"

Will's eyebrows shoot up. We're barely moving to the music anymore.

"Anyway, he breaks it off after two years of dating, dumping me in the kitchen in front of my boss, the caterers, the servers, everyone. And then he returns to the reception, leaving me embarrassed and on the verge of a full-on breakdown. My boss tells me to suck it up because I have to carry the groom's cake out. I tried to. I really did. But as I walked out there red-eyed, all I saw was Leo talking to some girl. It could have been his cousin, for all I know. But it didn't matter. It set me off again, and I started crying. We'd been together for ages, and I did not see it coming. I also didn't see the cords running along the floor until after I'd tripped over them and fell to the ground on top of the groom's cake before all the guests. Of course, I was fired after that—and told I was way too unprofessional to work with."

We stand there until Will starts swaying again, and I follow his lead. "Whoa."

"Nope. Didn't stop there. After that, the video of my chocolaty face-plant made the rounds on social media, so I shut down my online cookie business and burned all my aprons. Not really. But I got rid of them."

"Cookie business? What do you mean?"

"Oh, I took orders online, mostly getting the word out on social media, and made specialty cookies for events and parties and stuff." I fiddle with his collar. "It was small-time. But I stopped a couple of months ago after the incident."

"Let me get this straight. Because of this one thing, you gave up your dream of owning a bakery? Even though you were already working on it?"

"Well, yeah. It was traumatic. The bakery owner said some brutal things."

He shakes his head, and we slow to a stop. "You can't give up. That's crazy."

The same defensiveness bubbles up. My parents continually bring it up. I'm so tired of hearing it.

When I don't respond, he says, "Come on. Make those cookies for Ava. She'd love it, and I'll help you."

My frown deepens. I drop his hand and step away. "Now you sound like Fran. You're trying to get me to do more things I don't want to do? That's pushy. And it's not your business."

He runs a hand through his curls. "Guess not."

I walk over to our table and kick off my heels. Will's footsteps scrape behind me. "I'm sorry. I didn't mean to make you mad. I was just trying to encourage you."

"Look, Will"—I bend to loop a finger through the strap of my shoes—"it's fine. I'm having a bad night. I —"

My phone starts vibrating on the table, and Leo's song plays at a high volume—another person trying to bend me to their will.

Will glares at Leo's name on my screen, then steps back. I get the sense he's waiting for an answer to some question I didn't know he was asking.

I grab it off the table, reaching for any excuse to get away. "I need to take this."

20

Will

The summer breeze blows through my hair as Morgan saunters away, phone glued to her ear. My palms sting where my nails dig in. She laughs at something Leo says, the sound drifting back and twisting my gut.

"Hey, man. You good?" Hudson claps my shoulder, face pinched.

I force a smile. "Yeah, of course."

Emma and Ava join us, wearing matching frowns rather than the earlier bridal-party shirts.

"What was that about?" Ava waves toward where Morgan disappeared into the darkness. "Who's she talking to?"

"Leo." At least, I manage not to spit the word out like a curse.

"Ah," says Ava unhelpfully.

Hudson crosses his arms. "Maybe you should go after her and—"

I hold up a hand. "Stop. Please. I'm fine. It's not a big deal. In fact, this is how it should be, just as I told you." I give a careless chuckle. "Setups never work."

Hudson starts to say something else, but Ava grips his arm. He closes his mouth. She lowers to the pavilion's edge, unbuckles her sandals, and wiggles her toes. "We won't pester you anymore. Just know, Leo was always going to keep calling and texting. Morgan needed to hash it out with him. She could've picked a better time to do it, but her retreat wasn't about you." She shrugs and stands, her shoes dangling from her fingers. "Now, let's forget about that. Who's ready to get to work?"

I'm thankful for the subject change, though Morgan's anger over those stupid cookies *was* about me.

The music has stopped, signaling the end of the rehearsal, and the guests are dispersing. It's time to get this whole wedding business done and go home. I slap my hands together. "What still needs to be done? Put me to work."

Grimacing, Ava pulls the list from her clutch. "Well, we need to string up the rest of the lights. The boxes are at Evelyn's place." She sets her shoes in a chair. "We also need to rearrange the tables. The caterers cleaned up pretty well, but we'd better give it a once-over. And we also need to arrange the tables at The Meeting House for brunch tomorrow."

I loosen my collar. "How about I take the golf cart and get the lights?"

Hudson nods. "I'll grab the ladder."

"Emma." Ava unclasps her gold bracelet and places it by her shoes. "Want to help me move these tables?"

"Sure."

We head off in opposite directions. Most of the older adults have made themselves scarce.

I jump from the concrete slab onto the grass and jog to the golf cart. I don't notice Morgan until I'm driving away. She's sitting on a step near the dock, deep in conversation on her phone. I tear my gaze from her where her long flowing dress cascades over her legs and loose tendrils from her bun sway in the breeze.

Sure, she's attractive and sweet and funny. But that doesn't mean it's meant to be. I may have let my meddling cousins talk me into thinking about the possibilities, but look where that got me—left standing on the dance floor like an idiot as the beautiful girl strolls away to talk to another guy.

I drive up the dark hill. Moonlight glints across the lake's surface. Just another twenty-four hours. Back home tomorrow night, I can reconnect with the guys and find out about the rest of the trip. Pack my room for college.

So why can't I keep from wondering how Morgan's conversation is going? Is she telling him to stop calling? Or…not?

Let it go, Will. Let it go.

When I return with a box of lights, Ava, Morgan, and some of the bridesmaids have gone to The Meeting House. The rest of us will finish the pavilion.

We're about to turn in for the day when Fran returns, waving her arms as she clicks her heels up the steps. "Boys. Boys. I have the best idea."

"Oh?" A wary tilt deepens Hudson's voice.

"I'd like all of you to join us for the bridal brunch. Not to eat, of course, but you can be our servers." She claps. "It will make it so special for the girls to be waited on by you all. Oh, but not you, Hudson. You can't see the bride tomorrow until the wedding!"

I don't say anything, but a general grumble of assent rumbles around me.

"Wonderful. We'll see you at nine thirty at The Meeting House. The ladies arrive at ten. Don't forget to wear a suit and tie!"

And with that, she saunters away.

"I was hoping to sleep until noon tomorrow," someone whispers.

My thoughts exactly.

21

I trail the other groomsmen on our short trek up the boardwalk to brunch. I'm already pulling at my collar, my tie choking me. At least it's a beautiful day. And the last day of this wedding fiasco. No matter what happens, all will be done tonight.

We arrive five minutes late, much to Fran's annoyance.

She provides a clipped rundown of what we will do over the next few hours. Our first task is to escort the ladies to their assigned seats around the table. And judging by the number of place cards, many more females—family and close friends—have arrived.

Emma and Mema push through the flower-lined gate first.

But before I can offer my arm, Fran swoops in to ensure everyone knows she's in charge. "Will, be a dear and escort your grandmother to her seat." She snaps her fingers. "Matt, you take Emma."

When Fran leaves us, I catch Emma's eye, and we both make a face.

"Don't speak ill of others," Mema chides, trying to hide a smile.

Emma looks over her shoulder at us. "We didn't say anything."

"I know you two. You had a whole conversation with your eyes."

Emma giggles as she takes Matt's arm.

Once I've safely delivered Mema to her seat, I return to the entrance where Fran is greeting Ava's great-grandma Thompson.

"Will, this is my husband's grandmother, Glenda Thompson."

I offer my arm to the tiny white-haired woman, and she squeezes it lightly.

"You look lovely today, Mrs. Thompson," I say as we shuffle at turtle speed to the table.

Her cheeks lift, and her soft hand pats my wrist. "Thank you, dear. Such a nice young man."

Smiling, I pull out her chair. Then Morgan's at the entrance. Her hair shines golden in the morning sunlight. Soft curls flow over her shoulders and blue sleeveless sundress.

Is she watching me get Mrs. Thompson settled? As I make my way back, there's something unreadable in her eyes.

"Morgan!" Fran descends. "How lovely to see you. I'm so glad you fixed your hair today."

Morgan's expression hardens, but Fran only snaps her fingers at me. "Will, dear, please take Morgan to her seat."

"Morning." I offer her my arm. I might have tried to avoid her, but there's nothing for it now. "Sleep okay?" There, I'll pretend everything is normal. But things aren't normal, and when she takes my arm, I'm too aware of the light pressure of her fingers through my suit jacket. Her touch zings clear to my core. Stupid.

A wry smile twists her lips. "Not really."

Was she up late talking to Lenny? Not that I care. "Long phone conversation?"

Her grip tightens, perhaps on reflex. "Longer than I would have liked. But, no. I had a lot on my mind."

I shouldn't zero in on the words *longer than I would have liked*. Still, I'd love to know what was on her mind.

I. Don't. Care.

I don't *want* to care. It's none of my business.

Luckily, before I can blurt more questions, my sister, Sophia, rushes over and grabs my free hand, shoving my suit sleeve up my arm. "You're still wearing it."

I shake her off. "Of course. I told you I would."

She runs off yelling, "Brooklyn, I told you he was wearing the bracelet I made."

Morgan says nothing, but her gaze is soft. Her lips twitch like she wants to smile. I want her to smile.

No. I pull my sleeve over the bracelet.

I. Don't. Care.

As I deliver her to the table, Fran trots over and shoves something in Morgan's hand. "I think you need this, dear." She points at Morgan's face. "Concealer for the bags under your eyes."

Morgan's mouth falls open, and the little bottle shakes in her hand. But before she can say anything, Fran flits away across the stone patio, balancing like a pro on her spiked heels.

Horrible woman. Morgan's cheeks have pinked, and I swipe the bottle from her. "Give me that. You're the most beautiful girl here. And for the record, I liked your hair yesterday."

Yikes. The words have left my mouth and are out there between us.

Morgan's eyebrows shoot high on her forehead.

My mouth hangs open as if I could breathe the words back in. I shrug and pocket the bottle. "She's the worst."

The corners of Morgan's mouth lift. "She really is… and, um, thank you."

I bolt away the second she sits. Why can't I keep my mouth shut?

I blame Fran for being so blunt. I was protecting Morgan. That's all. We're friends. Sort of.

I hiss out a breath, grab a pitcher of fresh orange juice, and make the rounds, filling glasses upon request as the other groomsmen usher the rest of the ladies.

Matt seats Ava next to Morgan, and when I top off their juice glasses, Ava says, "Wow, Will. Looking sharp."

"Thanks." My chest puffs. Morgan's watching me again, smiling again. I continue around the table. But the phone call plagues me, and Morgan's words—*longer than I would have liked*—play, stuck on repeat.

Then Fran calls us groomsmen back into The Meeting House, where we take trays from the bewildered kitchen staff who can't be used to guests bringing their own suit-clad servers.

Balancing plates of quiche and fruit, I ferry them to the long table.

As I pass behind Morgan's chair, Ava tilts her way. "He said he wants to see you? What did you say?"

I slow. But they lower their voices, and I must continue to the other end of the table.

Maybe they're not even talking about *him*. But, then again, perhaps this is the answer to my question. That phone call went well, and she wouldn't be talking about seeing him if she wasn't thinking about it.

A squeal arises from Fran, who's standing at the head of the table. All heads turn her way. "Look who made it!"

She rushes to the gate to let in another woman about her age. They hug, and Fran leads her to the table.

"Everyone, this is one of my dear friends, Karen Pax. I wasn't sure she could make it, but here she is."

"Oh, we wouldn't miss it, honey," the woman drawls in her thick country accent.

"We? Did you bring a date?"

"No, no. Leo insisted on joining me. The dear. He didn't want me to have to come alone."

Did she say Leo?

Morgan's eyes are wide, but she's not looking at Mrs. Pax. She's looking toward the parking lot.

A tall, good-looking blond about our age stands in the gravel near her car. He waves and leans against the door like he owns it. Behind him, the faded remnants of blue ICEE are barely visible. With a dimpled grin, he points at it and mouths, "What is that?"

She shrugs and waves back.

If I wasn't sure before, I'm sure now. *Here's* my answer.

I grind my teeth, annoyed with Hudson for pushing me toward her. I chuck the concealer in the garbage and head for the gate.

It's time for me to clock out.

My time with the brunch crowd is over.

22

Morgan

Ava's bridal party chatters, several rising to greet Mrs. Pax, but all I can focus on is the beautiful boy—smiling at me and reclining against my car across the decorative fence separating us brunch-goers from the parking lot. My pulse has picked up into high gear.

Tonya slides down a few seats and nudges my arm. "Is that Leo? He's yummy."

I nod, not trusting my voice.

"I'm surprised he came." Ava flicks my hand. "Did you know he would be here?"

Leo smiles even wider, enjoying our attention.

"No." My insides are ajumble. "We talked yesterday, but he didn't mention it."

What will my parents think about him being here?

What do I think?

What will Will think?

I shift in my seat. Will's no longer where he stood only a moment ago. He's pushing through the patio gate.

I open my mouth to call him back, but what would I say?

The maid of honor whispers, "Things. Just. Got. Interesting."

I sigh. "I don't know about interesting. But complicated."

Ava lets out a low whistle. "Oh, it's interesting. That's for sure." She grabs her phone. "I have to text Hudson."

"Don't." I grip her hand, stilling her. "Please. Besides, you promised you wouldn't communicate today until you see each other at the altar."

"Fine." She huffs and clatters her phone to the wooden tabletop. "But guess what we're going to whisper about while the minister is talking." She flashes a devious smile, and Tonya laughs.

"Ava," I scold.

"I'm kidding, of course."

Fran stands and taps her knife against her third mimosa. "Ladies, ladies, can I have your attention."

Tonya returns to her seat, as do the other ladies who had begun milling about the patio.

Once Fran has waited a beat too long, ensuring she has every eye upon her, she continues. "This morning, we celebrate my dear Ava. What a glorious time for all those who love her to gather together."

A general murmur of ascent rises.

Fran gestured toward her daughter. "Ava, dear, would you, first, like to say a few words to your guests? And then perhaps tell them some of your love story."

Ava stands, gripping her napkin. My poor friend wasn't expecting this. Fran waves her to the front, jittery with excitement. Only someone truly oblivious to the inner workings of an introvert would put one on the spot like this. If there's any word that describes Fran, it's oblivious.

Here at this table, we're all friends and family, and though her cheeks are flushed, Ava moves to the head of the table and speaks with quiet confidence.

"I want to thank all of you for joining us today and some of you for the entire weekend. I'm so honored you have taken the time to travel to this lovely, albeit remote spot in Oklahoma that means so much to Hudson and his family and now to me as well."

Leo has moved on, and the pale-blue stain reflects the sunlight.

Ava gives me a wistful grin, then eyes my car. "And as far as my love story goes, I would love to tell you it was love at first sight, but it just wasn't. Love is messy. We all know that. I didn't even like Hudson at first. A true enemies-to-lovers story for those of you who read romance novels."

Emma, the in-resident romance author, puts her chin on her palm, a dreamy glaze in her eyes. "My favorite trope."

We laugh at this.

"Sure." Ava flips a lock of her blonde hair over her shoulder. "He was cute, but it took me a while to work out my feelings and give it a chance. I told myself, 'Hey, there's something between us, and I'm not sure what it is. It might be nothing, but it might be something.'" She lifts a shoulder. "Turns out it was something."

"And the rest is history," Fran croons, wiping her eye, but I doubt there's moisture there.

Ava slides in next to me and jostles my shoulder. "That little speech was for you."

"I know. Good job, by the way. Not the pointed content. The delivery."

Fran's mother speaks next, followed by several other family members. Each tell Ava how much they love and admire her, adding in their own brand of marriage advice and well wishes.

When brunch ends and everyone drifts away from the patio, Ava elbows me. "Someone hopes to catch you on your way out."

Leo's waiting at the gate, leaning against the fence.

"Oh man," Emma says. "I hope you don't have some sort of love triangle going on here. *Not* my favorite trope. But if you do, know I'm firmly on Team Will."

I roll my eyes and stand. "I better see what he wants. I'll catch up to you ladies in a while."

"Have fun."

"Right."

Leo flashes the charming dimpled grin that used to make my knees weak. "Hey, you."

"Hey." I grip my fingers together behind my back, suddenly tired. "You didn't tell me you were coming."

Dimples deepening, he runs a hand through his tousled blond hair again. "I told you I wanted to see you."

"Kind of a long drive."

"Not that long. But that might be because I slept most of the way." He shrugs. "Can we go somewhere to talk? Maybe take a walk?"

I hesitate but agree to a short loop up the hill.

As we stroll down the sidewalk, sunlight filters through the trees and houses, kids speed by on bikes, and a light breeze tickles my face and arms. "It's the perfect day for a wedding."

We engage in mindless small talk until we pass Firefly Park, a tiny green area hosting well-manicured trees. Teenagers lounge in hammocks, and their laughter floats our way. One of them even strums a guitar.

The serene morning mocks my mental turmoil.

I clear my throat. "Leo, what are you doing here? You've been calling and texting all weekend. You wanted to see me, and now we're face-to-face. What is it you want?"

The wind rustles his blond hair, and he shoves his hands in his pockets. "I don't know. I guess I–I miss you, Morgs."

I sidestep an abandoned scooter. "You miss me?"

He puts that grin back on his face, his dimples folding into his cheeks. "Well, yeah. I mean, it hasn't been the same without you this summer."

My breath catches in my throat. Part of me has missed him too. We'd been so close, once upon a time. But then he shattered my heart. "I don't know what to do with that right now."

"You don't have to do anything with it right now. Just think about it."

As I struggle with my conflicting feelings and what to say next, my phone chirps. My shoulders relax. "Ava's asking me to come back to start work on our hair and nails."

He frowns. "It's hours until the wedding."

"I'm learning wedding prep is no joke." I dim the screen and take a step away. "I should go."

His frown deepens. We've barely had a chance to talk, and I know these few words have not satisfied everything he has to say. "Want me to walk you back?"

"That's okay. I need to think."

"Okay, but text me if you have more time this afternoon. I'm around."

"I will." But deep down, I know I won't.

My mind spins with jumbled thoughts. I point my feet back down the hill toward the rental house.

Memories play, and none involve Leo. For once, I'm not replaying all our good times. Instead, the past two days warm me.

Will and our chance meeting at the gas station. Our shared secret. Our mutual hatred of Fran. Our laughter when he toppled off his paddleboard and the electric moment that followed. And our fantastic kiss in the jewelry store. No doubt something's there. Or there was. Before I sabotaged it.

I've been keeping him at a distance because I feared he'd be like Leo and every other immature boy I know. But he's not. He's not pushy. He's been helping me. Encouraging me.

I'm the worst. At the house, I stomp onto the porch steps and wrench the door open. I sink onto the couch and drop my head into my hands.

I like him. I like Will.

There. I admit it. Admitting you have a problem is the first step. Or so I've heard.

And I do have a problem.

I like a boy I just met, and tomorrow, we're both going home to different cities.

It might be nothing. But what if it's something?

And thanks to my stupid no-dating-until-college rule and Leo's sudden appearance, I may have ruined everything before it began. Will probably thinks we're off making out somewhere.

I huff a sigh that turns into a growl, flop back on the couch, and count the ceiling beams. This is ridiculous.

I've known him for less than forty-eight hours! You can't like someone in that amount of time. What about the whole friends-first thing?

"Um, you okay?"

I startle and lift my head. Ava is standing at the island, partially hidden from view, steeping a mug of tea. I lie back down. "Oh, hey. I didn't see you."

"Clearly." She's smirking. "So—How'd it go?"

I groan again. "Ava, I'm an idiot."

She chuckles, not bothering to disagree. "What are you going to do about it?"

I don't know. And I'm saved from responding when the rest of the bridesmaids thunder downstairs.

"Time for nails!" Tonya plops a basket onto the coffee table.

Ava winks over her mug. This conversation isn't over.

23

Morgan

I wiggle my toes when Tonya finishes my nail polish, the shimmering pink a nice change from my usual neutral tones.

"Nice." I'm a little girl again, my babysitter and her bestie fussing over me. "Thank you."

Tonya twists the cap on the bottle. "No problem. I'd love to put a flowery decoration on them, but Ava wants them all the same."

"What the bride wants, the bride gets."

Ava and the other bridesmaids have already finished up and are bustling around. Grandma Thompson surprised us with wood-fired pizzas from Mama Tig's, assuming we'd be hangry way before we got to eat again at the reception. Smart woman.

Ava's nibbling on a slice, pacing and muttering about everything that needs to be done and what might be forgotten now that Evelyn is out of the picture. She's starting to stress again. I've been preoccupied and need to focus on the bride.

I'm about to ask her if I can do anything. Then stiffen. Fran's lurking on the porch, phone pressed to her ear. I lean toward Tonya and pitch my voice low. "What's she up to now?"

Fran seems to be growing more agitated with every gesture and clipped word.

"Who knows?" Tonya makes a face. "But I feel sorry for whoever she's talking to."

"Right?"

Fran shades her eyes and peeks in the window.

Tonya waves at her and whispers, "Oh man, she is exhausting." She cringes. "Oops. Did I say that out loud?"

I laugh. "Ava didn't hear. She's wandering away up the stairs."

Apparently, this is the moment Fran was waiting for. She rushes inside, nearly tripping on the rug, but it doesn't slow her down.

She hovers over us and whispers, "Shh, don't react. The photographer just called. His car broke down halfway here. He's not going to make it in time for prewedding photos! And what if he doesn't make it at all?"

"What did you say?" Ava screeches in high pitch as she descends the stairs, her phone in hand.

"Oh, honey." Fran straightens. "I'm sure he'll make it for the actual wedding. He just has to."

Ava's shoulders sag, and the crease between her eyebrows sinks deeper than ever. When she reaches the bottom step, she slumps onto it. "What's happening? Is this and everything else a sign? Am I making a mistake getting married this weekend?"

"No!" Tonya, Fran, and I say in unison. We rush to her, sitting around her in a protective circle.

Tonya rubs her back. "Everything is going to be fine. You guys are meant to be together. Either it's a huge unfortunate coincidence or Satan's at work trying to keep a perfect pair apart, standing, as always, between anything wholesome or lovely. Don't let doubt creep in. You're getting married tonight…and just think of all the stories you can tell your kids someday about your wedding."

Ava laughs through a sniffle, and everyone starts to relax.

Tonya pushes Ava's hair behind her shoulders. "Plus, we can all take pictures with our phones before the ceremony and while we get ready. We're on it."

There's a murmur of agreement, and Ava nods, wiping her tears with her sleeve. "But what if he doesn't make it by the time the ceremony starts?"

"I'm sure he will, honey," Fran says.

"Wait a minute." I straighten. "What about Will and Hudson's cousin Emma? She has her camera, remember?"

Ava lifts her head and meets my gaze, her features softening.

I squeeze her shoulder. "She could take photos of us getting ready until he arrives."

Fran is nodding like a bobblehead. "And she could be the backup for the wedding if it comes to that! Oh, this is lovely. Ava, do you have her number?"

"No, but I have Will's. He could text her."

Ava lifts her phone. She's still for a moment. A slow smile widens her lipsticked mouth. She taps away, a glint in her eye. "I need to run up and finish something. Morgan can call Will. I just sent his number to your phone."

Wait. What? "You could have texted him in that time!"

Fran stands, clapping her hands again. "Okay, enough tears! No puffy eyes for the wedding! Ava, hand over the list."

Ava shrugs and fishes it from her pocket and turns it over.

Fran smooths the crumpled paper on her slender thigh. "Let's get back to business, ladies. One final push. I need all hands on deck. Morgan, fetch your phone. Tonya, double-check that everything is in order at the pavilion."

She runs a finger down the list and assigns various tasks.

"Unbelievable," I whisper to Ava. "I thought you had something you needed to do."

"Hey, at least now you have his number." She winks and gives my back a push. "You heard the woman. Fetch your phone!"

I roll my eyes, leaving her on the step, and grab my phone from the coffee table. Sure enough, there's Will's number. An army of butterflies takes flight in my stomach. He won't answer. No one answers unknown numbers. I put his contact information in my phone and call anyway.

After three rings, I'm about to hang up when I hear, "Hello."

I gasp, momentarily stunned.

"Morgan?"

"Oh, sorry. I didn't expect you to answer. Wait. How did you know it was me?"

"Um, Hudson put it in my phone earlier."

Right. The matchmakers.

"What's up?" He rushes on, his voice clipped. "Do you need something?"

I tell him about the photographer and my idea. "We're hoping either Emma's with you or you have her number so you can ask her."

"Sure. I have it." All business. "I haven't seen her in a few hours because her sisters arrived. But I'll text her now."

From the door, Fran is waving at me. "Come on. You can join Ava and me at the chapel to meet the florist."

"Fran?" Will says.

"Yeah."

"Sorry."

"Yeah." I let out a breath and follow the mother of the bride out the door. "It sounds like we're going to the chapel if Emma wants to meet us there."

"All right. I'll tell her."

"Thanks, Will."

"Yep." The call ends as if he couldn't wait to cut me off.

I can't blame him.

Fran, Ava, and I load into the golf cart. Fran drives while Ava and I sit shoulder-to-shoulder in the back seat. At first, Ava leans forward, chattering about the wedding details with her mom, but eventually, she scoots back and gives me a wicked grin. "So…what did Will say?"

"He said he'd ask Emma."

"Of course he did. Did he say anything else? Anything more interesting?"

I cross my arms. "No."

Her eyes twinkle. "Too bad."

Yeah. Too bad.

The florist is already unloading, so we pitch in to help. I carry a lovely arrangement of white roses accented with two types of smaller blue flowers that Ava explains are called delphinium and forget-me-nots.

She nudges me when we return for our second load. "Look who it is."

Will and Emma are walking down the boardwalk. Emma holds her camera with one hand and waves with the other.

Will avoids my gaze and addresses Ava. "I heard you needed a photographer."

Ava rushes to Emma. "Thank you. Thank you. You're a lifesaver. Are you sure you don't mind?"

"Not at all. I'd love to."

"Thank you so much."

As we lift boxes of flowers from the florist's van, Emma edges in closer to Ava. "So…how's everything inside? Is the archway these two put together still standing?"

My mouth drops open, and Will glares at her.

Ava only laughs. "Yes. Everything is good. The florist is decorating the archway now."

Emma winks, and rubbing the back of his neck, Will finally meets my eye.

I pretend to wipe sweat from my brow. "Whew."

At least, Emma didn't tell Ava about the leftover piece. Instead, she snaps photos as Ava and Fran make sure the florist knows what to do. Emma and I carry flowers to Tonya at the pavilion, and Emma explains her plan to capture a brief send-off message from each person in the bridal party. I love the idea and promise to let her record mine later. But what'll I say?

Will returns to the other groomsmen, and Emma accompanies to capture their prewedding shenanigans.

I never had a chance to talk to him. It seems he didn't want to anyway.

On my way back to the chapel, I pull out my phone and shoot him a text.

Morgan: Thank you. Emma's going to do a great job.

When he replies with a thumbs-up, I frown at my phone.

Ava waves me over to the golf cart where she's waiting for Fran to stop micromanaging the florist.

I slide in next to her.

She nods at my phone. "Leo?"

"No. Will."

"Why the frown?"

I lift a shoulder and show her the short conversation. "He's done talking to me. Or even looking at me, for that matter."

A crease sinks into the skin between her brows. "You never told me how your talk with Leo went."

"It was all right."

She lets out an exasperated breath as the breeze rustles her hair. "Morgan. Details. He didn't come all this way to accompany his mom. What did he say?"

"Fine. He says he misses me."

She sits straighter. "I knew it. And do you miss him?"

I rest against the seat. "No. Not at all." It's entirely true. "I mean, I did for a while. But not anymore."

Ava shoves her hair aside and rests her elbows on her knees. "So, not a love triangle after all." She winks. "Enemies to lovers it is."

She'd be right if my life were a romance. But it's not. Lately, it's just a series of unfortunate events leading up to an overly complicated wedding. What do you call that kind of story?

"Ava, he doesn't like me. He won't even talk to me. And no wonder. I've been pushing him away since I got here. And now Leo's here. And everything is complicated."

"But here's the question. Do you like Will? And I don't want to hear any of your crap about not dating until college."

I splay my fingers, palm up, in my lap. "Yes. I like him. But I've only known him for, like, what? Forty-eight hours?"

Her phone buzzes. An unknown number flashes. She lifts it where I can't see and opens the text. Her eyes go wide. "Morgan Whitney, you've been holding out on me."

"What?" I reach for the phone, but she jerks away. She starts reading the text aloud. "'Hey, Ava. This is Emma. I know this is weird. Your future husband didn't want to break the no-communication rule of the day, but he just had to share these photos with you. He found them in his glove box.'"

I slap a hand over my mouth. "Oh no," I say behind my fingers. I can't keep from smiling and blushing, so I try to hide both with my hands.

"Oh no, is right." Ava sings out a laugh. She pushes to her feet next to the golf cart as if the news is too big to take sitting down. "Why didn't you tell me about this?"

When she turns the phone around, I peek between my fingers. There on her screen is a photo of one of the Polaroids I hid in Hudson's truck. The one of that amazing kiss. Will's hand on my neck. His thumb brushing my jaw. My hand gripping his shirt. Our lips pressed together.

Another photo flashes onto the screen, and I lower my hands. This one, now that I look at it, may even be more intimate than the last. Our bodies are standing in the same position, but our lips have separated. Our faces are very close, and we're staring at each other with an odd, dazed shock.

It wasn't just me. That kiss surprised him too.

Ava must've seen the change in my face. She pulls the phone back and lets out a little yelp. "I ask again. Why didn't you tell me about *this*?"

"We agreed not to. We thought you'd make a big deal out of it." I wave my hand up and down in front of her. "Like you are right now. They wouldn't give us the ring until we kissed for the photo."

She bounces on her toes. "Wow. This is too good. I guess that makes you a really good friend. To kiss someone you don't even like to get my fiancé's ring. But that's not really the truth either, is it? It wasn't someone you don't like after all."

She can't stop smiling.

I groan and put my head in my hands. "Ava, what do I do?"

She jams a hand on her hip. "Well, you have to tell him how you feel, obviously."

24

Will

I pull at my collar as I sit on a step outside the chapel. Hudson paces in front of me, wearing a charcoal suit, and he can't seem to stop fidgeting with the white rose of his boutonnière.

It's fifteen minutes until go-time.

He's a ball of nerves. Apparently, the feeling's catching.

"Dude. You're making me nervous." I shake out my jitters. "You good? You're not thinking about running, are you?"

He slows and gives me a look. When I grin, he relaxes his shoulders, and the corners of his mouth turn up. "No. No way. Just nervous. Big moment and all."

"Understandable. Everyone *will* be staring at you."

"Yeah. Thanks for that."

"No problem." I lean back and peek through the cracked doorway. "Looks like it's almost time."

The other groomsmen are seating the last of the guests in the elegantly transformed sanctuary. The archway Morgan and I assembled is unrecognizable, adorned with white roses and an assortment of blue flowers that cascade down its sides. As guests file in, a string quartet plays soft music, lulling everyone into a peaceful calm—well, everyone except Hudson and me.

"You better get up in case Fran comes back and catches you sitting out here in that suit."

"Nah, she won't be back. They're about to escort her to her seat." But I stand up anyway. Just in case.

"I need a distraction. Let's talk about something other than the wedding. Let's see what can we talk about?" He taps a finger to his lips, pretending to think. "Oh, I know. The photos I found in my truck."

I groan. Earlier, I faked an errand to escape his teasing. He'd shown all the groomsmen, Emma, even Mema. And I'm sure Ava confronted Morgan after Emma sent her the photos. Who knows how *that* conversation went.

"Don't start. You've embarrassed me enough for one day."

"Okay, okay. But just between you and me. How was it? The kiss, I mean."

I draw in a slow breath, waiting for his taunts to continue, but then let it out when they don't. "It was… good."

He slides his phone from his suit jacket's inner pocket, locates the photo, and then waves it in front of my face.

"Okay, fine. It was really good. There. Are you happy? I said it."

He tucks his phone away. "Yes, actually. I'm happy for many reasons." He peeks into the sanctuary, and I follow his gaze. "You need to ask her out, but we'll circle back to this conversation in a week or so."

He returns to pacing, and I roll my eyes. He'll never give up. I continue to scan the room until I scowl at a tall boy with an annoyingly charming smile.

"What? What's wrong?"

"There he is. This is why there's no need to revisit the Morgan conversation. I can't ask her out. She's still hung up on what's his name. The pretty boy." I gesture toward Leo chatting up guests.

Hudson scowls. "What's he doing here?"

"*She* invited him. Why else would he be here?"

"I don't know. The last I heard, she's not a big fan of the guy. Maybe he just showed up. And if I'm right, you have to stay and see how things play out. You're not still planning to leave after the reception, are you?"

"We'll see." I trail off, not quite believing his theory. She had to have invited him.

The music crescendos, and the other groomsmen join us.

We take our places next to Hudson on our side of the archway, facing a chapel of friends and family and breathing in the white roses' scent.

The photographer must've arrived because a man I don't recognize snaps away on a fancy black camera.

My mind wanders while the song comes to a close. Maybe I *should* talk to Morgan. Find out for sure what's going on with Pretty Boy.

When the guests stand and pivot toward the back of the sanctuary, Leo smiles and winks at someone I can't see, though I know who it is.

Maybe not.

The music changes, and my chest tightens when Morgan appears between the open doors. The evening sunlight streams around her as she leads the bridesmaids on their slow procession. Her silvery blue dress flows around her, and her bouquet of white and blue flowers perfectly matches the room. Her long, golden-brown hair, though partially pinned back, still cascades over her shoulders. Her warm brown eyes peer over her pink cheeks. She ducks her chin as everyone stares.

She's breathtaking.

Those cheeks lift into a smile, and I return the gesture before she takes her spot on the archway's other side.

The other bridesmaids and Ava make their way down the aisle, and the minister begins.

The ceremony flies by in a blur of vows and rings. The bride and groom are pronounced husband and wife, and we file out to congratulate the happy couple. Once the sanctuary clears, we return for photos and then follow the guests to the reception.

The lake glitters. The sun is low, promising a fantastic Oklahoma sunset. The strung lights are already twinkling around the pavilion, showcasing our hard work over the last two days.

I'm seated at a table with various family members while Morgan dines with her parents and an assortment of other guests. Leo's at another table with his mother. Good. He cranes his neck to glimpse Morgan. Of course, so do I, so I turn around to my dinner.

After a while, Emma saunters over and captures clips for her send-off video from my family. I'm not ready to deliver mine, so I tell her I'll do it in a little while.

"Will, I just heard about the wedding planner fiasco," my mom says from across the table as she cuts the last bit of her chicken. "You didn't tell me you had to work so much this weekend. I'd hoped the lake time would be fun since you had to miss part of your senior trip. Has it been terrible?"

Mema snorts a laugh.

Mom eyes her. "What?"

"Will has had a fine time from what I've seen in photos." Mema winks, and my mouth drops open. No. Don't say it. I beg her with my eyes.

Mom blots her lips with her napkin. "What do you mean?"

"You should ask him about Morgan."

"Oooh, who's Morgan?" My sister, Sophia, jumps all over this. "The girl you were dancing with last night?"

Mom elbows Mema, but Fran takes the mic, saving me from explaining anything or pointing her out. But then Fran says, "Morgan? Morgan Whitney?"

Everyone quiets.

Morgan reluctantly waves from where she stands with her parents near the dessert table.

My other sister, Brooklyn, points. "There she is. It is the girl you danced with!"

Thanks, Fran.

Fran gestures for Morgan to follow, so she obeys and follows the older woman out of the pavilion and to a hut that serves as the kitchen. I track her movement until the door closes behind her.

The reception returns to full volume, and my brows knit together. Oops. Mom and Mema are watching me with matching grins.

"Yes, Mom, that's Morgan."

Mema fans her hand at me. "Well, go save her from *that* woman."

I shake my head. "Morgan can take care of herself. Besides, I thought you said not to speak ill of anyone."

"Oh, pishposh. You know very well I could've used any number of adjectives there."

When I chuckle and pretend to zip my lips together, she pats my hand. Then Mom and Mema drift off to the dessert table, but my attention keeps returning to the hut.

They're probably making Morgan do more work. And they'll put me to work if I go over there. I'm done volunteering.

It's not my problem.

I pick at the white tablecloth, letting out a long breath.

Fine. I'll go. But then I'm coming right back to this table.

25

Morgan

"Mrs. Thompson, I don't know if I can. I haven't done this kind of thing in a long time and definitely not on a real wedding cake."

I'm standing in the pavilion's kitchen where Fran and Mrs. Pax, Leo's mom, are troubleshooting a mishap. The wedding cake, a modest but beautiful three-tiered masterpiece, was bumped on the way over. One edge of the bottom tier took the hit, and apparently, the poor girl who made the delivery doesn't have a clue how to fix the smeared icing.

The last cake I decorated was the one I face-planted into because I was crying after being dumped by this woman's son.

Mrs. Pax pats my shoulder. "Oh, honey, this fear is childish. Leo and I have discussed it many times." The door creaks open as she squeezes my shoulder. "You have to fix the cake. Fran needs you to."

They've discussed this? About me?

"No, you don't," comes another voice. "You don't have to do it." Suddenly, Will is there, his fingers wrapping around my wrist, pulling me toward the door.

The two women start to protest, but he holds up a hand. "Give us a second."

We leave the cramped space, and he faces me, gripping my arms. "You okay?"

I nod. Tears are gathering, and since I can't bear for him to see me cry about this silly thing, I lean forward and press my forehead into his chest.

He freezes but recovers. "You don't have to do anything. You can tell them off and come back to the reception, or if you don't want to tell them off, I'll do it. Just say the word."

I think he would. He'd do it for me. The thought turns up a corner of my mouth. "Better not."

He drops his hold and steps back. "Yeah, you're right. We don't want to make a scene. But—we could make a run for it."

I show him my heels.

"I could carry you."

I give him a look, but I'm smiling now.

He scratches his nose where his sunburn has almost completely faded. "Right. We could create some sort of low-key diversion while the cake is cut. That way, no one sees the problem. Maybe something to do with fireworks, like Black Cats or something."

I shake my head and lift my palms. "Fresh out of fireworks."

"Well, that's pretty much all I've got in the way of avoidance."

His expression screams "you don't have to avoid this," but at least he doesn't say it out loud.

I already know.

I sigh. "We could always arrange for Fran to trip over the cake Morgan-style."

His mouth drops open before his laugh bursts out. "Yes! I was so hoping you were ready to joke about that."

"Don't get excited. For now, only I can joke about it."

"Noted."

I shift my feet and let my shoulders sag. "I have to do it, don't I?"

"You don't have to."

"I need to."

"You don't need to."

I meet his gaze. "I want to?"

He doesn't say anything, but yeah, this is what he expected from me all along. To face the challenge. To get back to the thing I love.

This is a different wedding—a different day. "But I'm not doing it for Fran."

He makes a face. "Understandable. She's the worst."

"She really is."

"Do you need anything from me?"

"Well, if they ask me to carry a cake out there—"

"I'm on it."

"Right. And if you're about to trip over something—"

"You'll let me know."

"Good."

"Ready?"

"Ready."

"I'll wait here."

I head inside and redistribute frosting using piping from the bakery van. I shift the flowers and rearrange the top tier so the dented edge is now on the backside. It's not perfect, but who's going to notice in the time it's wheeled out before they cut into it? I advise Fran to tell the photographer to ensure he's standing at the right angle to hide any imperfections.

"How's that?" I step back from my handiwork.

Fran scrutinizes the cake. "Oh, Morgan, this will do. I can only see it a tiny bit."

Wow. That's high praise from her.

I've missed this. This creative outlet that lets me use my talents to bring joy.

Sure enough, they ask me to help present the cake, and true to his word, Will volunteers in my stead. He doesn't even stumble.

The photos are taken, the cake is cut, and Ava is happy.

Afterward, Will meanders away, and my mom hugs me when I tell her about the fiasco. "Proud of you, honey. You saved the day."

Fixing a cake is hardly saving the day, but I let her say it all the same.

Fran claps, addressing the bride and groom. "Time for your first dance as a married couple."

The DJ gets things started with Hudson and Ava's song. Across the room, one of Will's sisters seems to be pushing him toward me. But he holds his ground and waits a minute or so as rehearsed and then starts in my direction, a perfect smile on his face.

But Leo beats him to my side. My ex snakes an arm around my waist and spins me onto the dance floor.

Will pauses, his easy smile disappearing.

I put a hand on Leo's chest, but he only pulls me closer, turning me away from Will. "Leo, let go. This dance is for the wedding party."

He glances around, not loosening his grip. "No, it's not. Look. Everyone's joining in."

He's right. Many other couples are gliding onto the dance floor. The crowd has hidden Will from view. I try to pull away and stretch onto my toes to see him, but Leo holds me tight, swaying to the music.

Other couples swirl around us, and I feel their gazes upon me. Ava watches with a questioning look, Hudson glares, and my parents frown. They're not Leo fans.

Leo leans into my ear. "Have you had a chance to think about us?"

I lower my heels and focus on the dimpled boy before me. "There is no us."

"There could be. There should be. I miss you, Morgs."

I blow a strand of hair out of my face. My hands are resting on his shoulders, but, really, what else was I supposed to do with them when he forced me into a dance? His expression is hopeful, and I have to set him straight.

But I'd like to find Will first.

I crane my neck, but I don't see him anywhere. So to Leo, I say, "Fine. Let's go over to the sidewalk. I don't want to go far."

Let's get this over with.

Fifteen minutes later, we're still arguing.

"What do you mean? I've come all this way."

"I didn't ask you to come. Remember? I told you I needed to think and focus on this wedding. But you show up here and tell me *you're* ready to get back together."

"Keep thinking if you need to. Just know I'm here. Right in front of you. I rode in the car for three hours to see you." He grips my forearms, his gaze more intense than I've ever seen. "We're perfect together. You know it's true."

"Leo." I pull my arms back. "We're not perfect. We never were. Nothing is perfect. Love is messy, and that's okay. But—"

"Okay, okay. Take some time. I can be patient."

He keeps talking, droning on about our perfectness, not letting me get a word in.

I've always thought he was most handsome with this determined look. No doubt he's handsome now. It's a face that gets him far.

He's used to everything going his way and people doing what he wants. He probably never dreamed I might reject him.

I lift my palm to him. "Leo, stop."

He grabs my hand and kisses my palm as a new song begins. He grins. "It's our song."

I snatch my hand back. "No. Leo, it's over. Completely over. I don't need to think. We're done."

His smile fades. "You don't mean that."

"I do mean it. Accept it, please. We're not getting back together."

"But—"

"No buts." I pick up my long skirt. "I'm going to find my parents. Have a nice trip home."

I leave him standing there. Rejected—likely for the first time in his life.

I delete his ringtone and return to the pavilion. I find Hudson and Ava in a rare peaceful moment. No crowd of well-wishers surrounds them. I hug them both and congratulate them on how wonderful everything turned out.

"Well, almost everything," Hudson must be ready to burst with questions. Only Ava's holding them back.

I adjust one of the bobby pins securing my hair in place. "What do you mean?"

"Oh, come on. You knew I was rooting for Will." When Ava nudges him, he clears his throat. "But I guess these things don't always work out. That's life."

Ava smiles, trying to be upbeat. "So Leo. Where is he?"

I open my mouth. Close it. Cross my arms. "You think I got back with Leo."

"Well, yeah. That's what it looked like. Right? You danced with him instead of Will, all nice and cozy, and then you two disappeared for a while."

"It was not cozy, and that's just how long it took for his tiny brain to accept that I told him it was over. Forever."

"Oh." Hudson turns to Ava. "That's—"

She frowns back. "Unfortunate. Should we—"

"Yeah, probably." He pulls out his phone.

I splay my arms out wide. "I know you're having some sort of couples-only silent conversation, but remember, I'm standing here." I rise onto my toes and crane over the dancing mob again. "Where's Will? I need to talk to him."

Hudson makes a face. Ava ducks her head and fiddles with her hair.

"What?"

"Will...left."

I plop back onto my heels, eyes wide. "What do you mean?"

"He left. As in, went home. He was always planning to drive back after the reception. He said his goodbyes several minutes ago. He tried to find you for you, but you were…busy."

26

Will

I blast my family's Carlton Landing song as I cruise past Dollar General's glowing yellow lights. This song usually puts me in a good mood. Today, the beat falls flat. I grip my steering wheel, willing myself to put the evening's events out of my head.

I'm not mad, really. Neither Morgan nor I were open to the setup. In fact, we were both against it.

But there *was* a point when I thought things started to change. I guess not.

I pull into a gas station and begin filling my tank. Since there's only one on my path to the highway, I shouldn't be surprised to find myself at *the* gas station—the one where I met Morgan.

I lean against my car in the humid evening and glare at the spot where we crashed into each other. Would this weekend have been different if it hadn't happened? Would I still be at the wedding right now?

Or was she always going to invite Leo?

Loosening my tie, I shake the thought away. Eager for a painless exit, I didn't take the time to change.

With the gas tank full, I slide back in the car and drive over to a parking spot so I can zip inside for sunflower seeds and coffee.

I swipe my phone and freeze.

There's a missed call.

From Morgan.

My stomach twists, and I step from my car before swiping it onto my screen.

She didn't leave a message.

What did she want?

Should I call her back?

My fingers hover over the phone.

But I huff and lower it into my lap.

Or should I let it go? She didn't even leave a few words in my voicemail. She probably wants Emma's number or something. But she can get that from someone else.

Too bad we couldn't have parted on better terms and had a chance to say goodbye. Hudson said she was busy.

With *him.*

This thought solidifies my decision. I shove my phone into my pocket.

With the way I feel right now, I shouldn't talk to her. Even to say farewell. Not when I know Lenny is hovering over her shoulder.

On this happy thought, I go inside to select a package of pickle-flavored sunflower seeds. It's late, and those will help me stay awake when the caffeine starts to wear off. The stale odor of fried food and old coffee assaults me as I step into the empty station.

I have an hour and a half drive ahead of me, and I plan to make good time so I can stop by the pool party when I get into town. Hopefully, it goes until late. Scarlet hasn't been on my mind for days, driven out, of course, by Morgan. After the weekend, I don't want to pursue that possibility. But the party should be fun—something to look forward to anyway.

I approach the drink station and grab an insulated cup. The burned coffee smell turns my stomach. Maybe I should get a Dr Pepper instead.

As I start to put the cup back, movement catches my eye. I suck in a quick breath.

A beautiful girl in a flowing blue dress has burst through the front door. She's ditched her heels and lost the pins holding back her long hair. The locks flow around her face, and she shoves them aside. Her chest heaves as her neck cranes, peeking over the rows and rows of junk food.

The clerk frowns at her bare feet.

She stretches onto her toes.
She's looking for someone.
And my heartbeat ticks up a notch when she finds
me.

27

Morgan

Will stares at me, his lips parted.

I walk toward him, not sure what to say. My heart thunders, and my palms have started to sweat. I smooth out my dress to wipe them off. I never dreamed he'd still be here. Now that we're face-to-face, I'm wondering what comes next.

He's holding a coffee cup, so I stop at the ICEE station before I reach him. Not breaking eye contact, I pull a red-and-blue cup from the holder.

He watches, a crease forming between his brows.

I twirl the cup to keep from fidgeting. "I want you to know I didn't invite my ex to the wedding." The pink polish on my bare toenails gleams against grimy linoleum tiles. "I'm sorry for everything. For pushing you away. For being a grumpy work partner. For not punching Leo in the eye when he wouldn't let me go during that dance. I wanted to find you."

His feet shift on the linoleum floor.

When he makes no immediate comment, I pull the level on the awful frozen raspberry, the electric-blue stream spooling into my cup. "I keep wondering if things would've turned out differently if we'd met at the wedding—rather than here." I shut off the machine, grab a straw, and then take a tentative step in his direction.

He nods to my ICEE, and the corners of his lips tilt up. "Are you planning to dump that on me?"

I giggle. "No. But how about a do-over?"

He reaches over to pour coffee into his cup. "Okay. And I've been wondering the same thing. What if things played out differently? What if we hadn't 'bumped into' each other? But...I have to ask, where's Lenny?"

I wrap both hands around the ICEE, the cold seeping into my fingers. I lift a shoulder. "I don't know. I told him we're not getting back together. Ever." I take another step in his direction. "That's what we were discussing when you left. I wish you'd said goodbye."

He lets out a breath, running a hand through his curly hair. "Yeah, me too. But...Hudson said he saw you run off together."

"I needed to talk to him to make sure he understood where he stands. Which is far away from me."

Will starts to sip his coffee but makes a face and lowers it to the counter. "I owe you an apology too." He snags my drink and sets it aside. "I'm sorry for not saying goodbye. And for your skirt and shoes and for calling you a"—he pitches his voice low—"psycho."

"I forgive you. I already did."

"Yeah?"

"Yeah. Though I think the ruined clothes were a joint effort." I reach up and smooth his rumpled tie. "And just so you know, I don't think you're the rudest boy in the world. So, sorry for that too."

His dark eyes glow beneath those amazing eyelashes, and their edges crinkle up with his smile. "Forgiven. Done."

"Good."

"Good. So we can be friends?"

"Yeah. We can be friends." My cheeks warm. "But—"

He steps closer. "Yeah?"

I sigh, inching toward him. "Well, I guess you're right. We can only be friends because you don't do setups. Because they don't work."

He pushes a lock of hair behind my ear. "But if you think about it, we met before Hudson and Ava had a chance to introduce us. So…it can't be a setup."

"That's a good point."

"And what about you?" His fingers brush mine. "I heard you're not dating until college. That's a year away."

"I did say that, but mostly because I'm tired of high school boys." My hand wraps around his. "But you're not one of those, are you?"

He glances at my lips. "No, I'm not."

"Will."

"Yeah?"

"I like you."

"I like you. But"—he brings his hand to my face, thumb tracing my jaw—"I *hate* it when Hudson's right."

I rise onto my toes. "They'll never stop bragging about this."

We're both smiling as our lips meet. My eyes drift closed, and he wraps an arm around my waist, pulling me closer, crushing his boutonnière between us. I grip his white dress shirt, and we share our second perfect kiss right there between the ICEE machine and the coffee maker.

A throat clears behind us, and our lips part. But we don't jump away from each other this time.

"Young lady, I hate to interrupt, but I have to ask you to leave. No shirt. No shoes. No service." The clerk shakes his head, laughing a bit, and heads back to the counter.

"I'm so sorry," I call after him. "I'm going."

Will tightens his arm, leaning in. "He's absolutely right. I cannot believe you came in here barefoot. You're disgusting."

"I was in a hurry!"

He sweeps me into his arms, deposits me outside, and mutters "This is not better" before running back inside to pay for our drinks.

He returns carrying the ICEE. "I tossed the coffee, but maybe something blue for the bride?"

"Perfect."

He threads his fingers through mine. "Back to the wedding?"

I squeeze his hand. "I owe you a dance."

28

Morgan
Two weeks later…

"I can't believe that guy." I swipe mud off my leg as Will, Hudson, Ava, and I make our way up the sandy boardwalk, dripping wet and cackling about our bad luck.

Ava wrings out her blonde hair. "It's called the no-wake zone for a reason. There's supposed to be no wake!"

Shaking his floppy curls, Will grins. "At least we got a good hour in before the big splash."

Hudson lifts his paddleboard to carry it over his head while simultaneously trying to drain water from his ear. He almost falls off the boardwalk, sending us into another laughing fit.

After adjusting his double-sided paddle in one hand, Will threads his fingers through mine with the other. "Hudson, I told you to leave it at the beach. I'm going back for the others later."

Flexing his muscles, Hudson pumps the awkward load over his head. "I can carry it back."

"I never said you couldn't. I said you didn't have to."

"Whatever." He starts whistling a merry tune as he and Ava walk on ahead.

Will and I trail the newlyweds, hand in hand. The bright August sun warms our skin, and the soft breeze tunneling down our path between the houses carries a hint of knockout roses and wildflowers.

He squeezes my fingers. "You did well out there. Especially since it was only your second time."

"Thanks. It was fun." I bump him with my shoulder and raise my voice. "Especially when I stayed on my board…unlike the rest of you."

"Doesn't count if you sit down," Hudson calls over his shoulder and stumbles again.

We laugh.

I had a great time on the water today, but I never considered staying upright when I saw the blue speedboat rocketing toward the no-wake zone. I was on my knees in a flash. The others sought the challenge, claiming they could stay standing. Wrong.

Will releases my hand and slides an arm over my shoulder. "But you still ended up in the water."

Snaking my arm around his back, I lean into him. My fingers brush the waistband of his ridiculous catfish swim trunks—*"for old times' sake,"* he'd said. "True. But you didn't get the pleasure of tumping me."

"True," he grumbles.

After the others fell in, my smug expression inspired Will to swim in my direction, calling, "Your hair won't save you this time!"

And so, I shrieked and executed a horrific cannonball into the water before he could reach me. Will's startled face was worth the plunge, even if I hadn't planned to get my hair wet.

We'd intended a quick, dry paddle before lunch and don't even have towels.

But despite our soggy state, an unexpected warmth fills me. What a surprising end to a summer that started so poorly—a summer bookended by two very different weddings. Two weeks into the summer, I face-planted into a chocolaty mess, derailing all my future plans. But two weeks before it ended, I met someone who helped me get back on track.

Not only have Will and I stayed in near constant contact via text or phone but also I've relaunched my cookie business. I've even had a few back-to-school orders.

Last weekend, a week after Hudson and Ava's wedding, Will drove to Edmond for the day so we could go out on our first date. My dad only complained once that I broke my deal—again—not to date until I'm thirty.

The two of us made the trek into the city, where we explored the Myriad Gardens and had dinner on the canal in Bricktown. We wrapped up early for his hour-and-a-half drive back to Tulsa.

And this week, when Mema planned on coming to Carlton Landing for the last weekend of summer, he asked if the two of us could tag along. Ava and Hudson, back from their honeymoon, decided to join us for one last getaway before all of us got on with our lives on Monday. Them to their jobs, me to my last year of high school, and Will to freshman orientation at OU—almost an hour closer!

Mema's front door swings open as we tromp up the steps and onto her wraparound porch, our wet flip-flops slapping the wood panels.

"Well, don't you all look like a bunch of drowned rats." She props the door.

Hudson hefts the board against the porch railing, and though his arm muscles had started to tremble, he made it, holding the board over his head all the way up the hill. "Yep. We took a tumble."

"I can see that." She waves us along. "Come on in and dry off. Lunch is almost ready."

We file inside, wiping our feet on her welcome mat, and tell her about the "red-dirt bath," as Will calls it.

After a few minutes, I run upstairs, taking them two at a time to change clothes and throw my hair in a bun.

When I come back, they've moved out onto the screen porch with their homemade fish tacos. I grab mine, and Will motions me over to curl up next to him on the couch. He points up at the patio TV. "It's the send-off video. Emma just sent it."

I sit straighter. "Finally."

Hudson and Ava sit pressed together in an oversized chair as their guests' messages play. Ava dabs at her red-rimmed eyes, but she can't stop smiling.

Mema blushes when she sees herself give a heartfelt speech about enjoying every minute together. Hudson and Will's uncle advises them to join the boat club, my mom thanks Ava for being such a good friend to me, and Will's sister asks if she can spend the night with them in their new apartment sometime. The videos continue, some serious and some silly, until finally, Will and I are on the screen.

Next to each other on the couch, we lock gazes, grinning. This video was captured after our return from the second gas-station saga—so many memories. That night, we'd returned to the wedding—after washing the blue from my car—in time for one last slow dance before Ava and Hudson made their grand exit. The two of us had then walked out to the dock, where kids were playing, rushing back and forth down the sturdy wood planks.

But Emma had followed us out, eager to add our well-wishes to the footage. She'd even brought the untouched melted ICEE as a prop, saying it was part of our wedding story.

In the video, we're standing on the dock as the glow from the pavilion lights our faces. My blue bridesmaid's dress floats around me in the breeze. Will has lost his tie, and we reach for each other's hand as Emma zooms in on Will.

"Hey, Hudson and Ava," he says. "Congratulations, and I wish you all the best. Thanks, Hudson, for always letting your little cousin hang out with you and protecting me when the girls tried dressing me up for tea parties. You were and are the best big cousin…even though I'm taller than you now."

Across the porch, Hudson snorts.

Will's onscreen self continues as a kid darts past, feet pounding on the wooden planks. "And just so you both know. This"—he indicates himself and me—"is not a setup. You can't take credit."

Hudson pauses the playback, and he and Ava launch into a debate with Will about whether or not this statement is true. Mema and I laugh, and I, of course, side with Will.

Finally, Mema says, "Shush, let's see what Morgan has to say."

Hudson grumbles but restarts the video. I catch Will's eye, wondering how Emma decided to end it. The shot pans my way until I'm center screen, holding the ICEE. I lift it in a toast. "Hey, guys. Congratulations, and thanks so much for including me in your big day. Ava,

I'm so glad your parents bought the house next door all those years ago. You were always my much cooler next-door neighbor, and I looked up to you more than you'll ever know. You are more than my favorite babysitter—you are also my friend." I brush the back of Will's fingers with my own. "And thank you for all the great advice this week."

The camera zooms out, switching to slow motion when the playing kid darts past again. But this time, he tumbles into me, and the video freezes on our shocked faces as the shiny blue waterfall cascades onto Will and me.

Hudson and Ava yell out in surprise.

"What?"

"No way!"

"It happened again?"

Mema rocks back, giggling, and we're all shaking with laughter as Hudson plays the ending three more times.

Once we've caught our breath, I snuggle into Will, still smiling. He leans down, lips touching mine.

Ava was right.

Love is messy. It isn't perfect.

I'm not sure what this is just yet, but there's definitely something here.

It might be nothing.

But just maybe…it might be something.

* * *

WANT MORE FROM MORGAN AND WILL?

Type this address into a web browser to
Read a **BONUS SCENE!**
https://www.evaaustin.com/i-want-the-bonus-scene/

Dear Reader,

Thank you so much for reading this teen and young adult romance! It means so much that you gave *My Favorite Color is Your Something Blue* a chance.

Are you looking for more sweet romance books like this one? Me too! I'm always searching for books to suggest to my readers. Sign up for my newsletter, and I'll send book recommendations as I find them. (I'll also let you know when the next *Favorite Color* book comes out!) Visit www.evaaustin.com, and don't forget to follow me on Instagram.

If you have questions about this book, the next in the series, or writing, please email via the contact form on my website. I look forward to hearing from you!

- Eva

Acknowledgments

I want to thank my wonderful family for supporting me while I try something new! Thanks to my husband for being my biggest encourager. You're the one who consistently asked, "What's your next goal?" or "Did you meet your goal today?" Thanks for keeping me accountable!

Thank you also to my kids for encouraging me and putting up with writing weekends and holiday editing. I love you so much and can't wait to see what God has in store for you!

And a special thanks to my editor, Deirdre. You tell it like it is, and I love it!

Eva Austin is a fiction writer, author of young adult contemporary romances.

Eva holds a BS from the journalism and mass communication department of Abilene Christian University. She teaches digital art to high school students while also managing her growing website, bookseriesrecaps.com, and writing fantasy stories under the name Sara Watterson.

When not writing, teaching, or enjoying her kids' many activities, Eva likes reading on the back porch, drinking coffee, and hanging out with her super-cute hubby. She lives in central Oklahoma with her husband and three children.

Stay up to date by joining Eva's mailing list here:

https://www.evaaustin.com

Let's be friends:

https://www.instagram.com/eva.austin.author
https://www.goodreads.com/eva_austin